THE HOMICIDE HUSTLE

BY CHARLENE TORKELSON

Copyright © 2011 Charlene Torkelson
All rights reserved.
ISBN:0615476074
ISBN-13:9780615476070

This book is dedicated to all the dancers I have met, all the dancers I have danced with, and all those I have taught. In some form or another you are a part of this book. A piece of you is in each and every character and in each dance performed. You are a special group of people with unique talents. You have and always will be a part of my life. Since the first year I began ballroom dancing, I have worn a small gold band on my little finger signifying my dedication and connection to all the dancers in the world. This book is for all of you who have played such a significant role in my life. Thank you.

INTRODUCTION:

Tara, the multimillion dollar disco was extreme and supreme. The owners had taken no shortcuts in developing a place of beauty from the ornately carved solid wood front doors edged in polished brass to the smooth glass dance floors allowing movers and shakers to peer through the thick blocks below their feet to the patrons seated below. The entry way surrounded a fascinating floor to ceiling fish tank filled with colorful tropical swimmers. Everything was spectacular – and every news channel and newspaper front page picked this as the hot spot of disco ambiance.

Normally this downtown hideaway didn't come to life until office workers ended their day – around four o'clock. But today it was bustling at ten in the morning with dancers and cameras and loud pounding music. The DJ was seated behind a glassed in booth bouncing and twitching rhythmically to the beat of the sound while large cameras were manned throughout the club.

"People, I need you to do hustle movements behind the front principals that have large arm movements like sweethearts and overhead wraps. Small movements will not show well in photos," the man with the huge halo of curls was scurrying around pointing here and there as he checked out his own image in the mirrored panels before positioning himself in the middle of the crowd and looping his arm over a tall slender woman with a flopping disco tail protruding from her head. Edward Garrett was in his element. To the owner of the local dance studios, this day was a dream come true. They were shooting jacket covers for soon to be released disco albums. But by the end of the day something else would be shot – or rather someone else would be shot. It was a hustle shoot that would be more memorable than anyone ever imagined.

1

I.

Larry Underhill was a true professional. His hair was always perfect and his expensive three piece suit always without as much as a crinkle at the knees. Larry Underhill's coffee colored face always displayed a cheerful smile and his lapel a fresh colorful boutonniere. "I decided long ago when I started in this business to have a flower sent to my home every morning so I would look and feel my best each day," he would explain to his customers when they asked. And they always asked. It was his calling card so to speak.

Larry was in the business of marketing – billboards and other forms of visual advertisements were his specialty. He was the best. That's why he was called to the studio beneath the parking ramp in downtown Minneapolis. Owner Edward Garrett had decided now was the perfect time for a billboard advertising his dance studios. After all, disco was hot and partner dancing was about the biggest craze this country had seen in several years. The market was ripe, and it was his turn to pluck the fruit.

Standing outside the glass door at the base of the parking ramp's elevator, Larry straightened his tie and checked his reflection in the window. Then with a smile that showed his perfectly straight capped teeth, he crossed the concrete floor and opened the door.

Larry Underhill saw a tidy waiting area surrounding a doctor style reception desk and a magical glistening wooden dance floor beyond. Long narrow windows enticed business executives power walking in suit and athletic shoes from parked car to office to momentarily gaze at the swaying dancers drawing in the sunlight and drag out their secret ambitions. Larry felt that same haunting ambition as he heard the beat of the music and imagined the promise of new found romance when holding a woman in dance position.

Morgan Canfield on the other hand observed a tall well built African American man in a black pin striped suit with a deep red rose in his lapel. Morgan was not a beauty. In fact she was a stocky dishwater blond with no makeup, a poorly cut mop of hair, and wrinkled shirt and skirt in a bland beige. Morgan Canfield, however, had a sharp wit and could make even the most staunch sourpuss laugh with her sarcasm.

"May I help you?" she peered over a pair of reading glasses looking at this intruder from foot to head and back down again.

Larry Underhill widened his smile and stuck out his hand. "Larry Underhill," he pulled a card out of his pocket with his left hand and placed it delicately on the top of the chest high desk top.

Morgan stared at the hand, reluctantly shook it, and then glared at the rose. "OK, explain the flower and I'll let you in," she cracked without so much as a slight grin.

Larry touched the plump rose and tilted his head to breathe in the fragrance. "Every morning I open my front door with my steaming cup of coffee in hand and pick up my morning paper along with a boxed boutonniere. It's my morning ritual to get me ready for my day," Larry never took his gaze off Morgan's deep burrowing eyes.

"Would that work for me? Will I look as perfect as you if I follow your routine?" Morgan deadpanned.

"Couldn't hurt," Larry Underhill fired back this time without the glowing grin.

"Touché. You're in with me. Now, what can I do for you?" This time Morgan's face slid into a lopsided chuckle.

"I have an appointment with Edward Garrett. I'm with ABC Advertising," he moved his card closer to Morgan. She squinted at the tiny print cautiously.

"Well, Mr. Garrett will be late for your appointment, I'm afraid."

"You don't even know what time I have my appointment," Larry protested peering around for a clock that wasn't there.

"Doesn't matter. Whatever time you scheduled, Edward will be late. Edward is always late," Morgan said with a matter-of-fact firmness.

"I take it this has happened before," Larry said without a hint of frustration.

"Always," Morgan replied quickly and sharply. "See, no clock. That's so you don't know just how late he will be."

But at precisely eleven o'clock, the agreed upon appointment time, Edward Garrett flew in the back door, his ankle length camel wool coat flapping around his thin gangly legs. His narrow dark brown leather Italian pumps strode briskly in front of the mirrored wall on his way to the reception area. Without his usual pauses to look at his reflection and pat his curly toupee back into place, Edward Garrett picked up the business card on the desk top, put out his hand and announced firmly "Larry Underhill? Edward Garrett here."

"You must be Elvis or something," Morgan muttered with a wide eyed shocked look on her face.

"Just call me 'The King'," Larry whispered out of the side of his mouth without breaking his perfect smile.

"Shall we get down to business?" Edward shrugged out of his coat revealing a brown pin striped three piece suit that rivaled Larry's in style and crispness. "Like the rose. Very nice touch," he added as the two men retired to the office off the reception area.

II.

Edward Garrett was a complicated man. He had talent and charisma along with a violent temper and a strong attraction for vices. When asked what those vices were, any dance studio staff member could quickly rattle off a long list including alcohol, drugs, fear of aging, self centeredness, a love of money, and women. Especially women. On the other hand Edward Garrett had some extremely good qualities. Unfortunately, that list wasn't rattled off quite as quickly.

The two studios owned by Edward included the older studio at the bottom of the parking ramp in downtown Minneapolis. The other was a newer barn-like studio in a ritzy suburban neighborhood surrounded by high end shops and businesses. Despite its boxy no window features, it attracted a large number of wealthy hobnobs making it extremely successful even during the "drought". That would be the time when partner dancing was not a popular or faddish thing to do. Now, however, with disco at its peak, the studios in both areas were attracting people of all ages and all income levels. Dancing - especially the hustle - was the thing to do. And Edward Garrett wanted to be a part of this popular dance scenario.

The condo Edward owned was a block behind the downtown studio. He only had to walk to work and sneak in the back door from the parking ramp itself to slip through the tiny kitchenette into the ballroom. That he had been on time for this appointment with Larry Underhill was utterly amazing – another of his vices was tardiness. Larry Underhill and his business must mean a great deal to Edward for him to be so prompt.

Friday morning and a quick meeting with all of his studio managers would begin at noon. Mary Lou Smith, the suburban studio manager normally didn't worry about being on time. After all, Edward wouldn't be there. Today however, when she came in carrying a takeout coffee and a briefcase full of weekly charts and figures to hand over to Edward, she was surprised when Morgan pressed her finger to her lips and pointed to Edward's office. What was this? Edward was not only on time but early? There must be something wrong.

Mary Lou put down her brief case and frowned. Mary Lou Smith usually frowned so this was not out of the ordinary. With her short squat body poured into a boxy well worn navy suit – plain over an equally plain white blouse with Peter Pan collar – and unbecoming sensible shoes, Mary Lou was as tough as they get. She had been with Edward for about seven years now and managing the new studio for about two of those years. No one knew exactly how she had been given the job as manager of the studio. Granted it was her idea originally to branch out and find a wealthy suburb to locate a second studio. "Suburban people don't come downtown," she had said. And she was right. But when Edward announced his choice for manager, Mary Lou was not at the top of the list. That list quickly changed however when Mary Lou had a behind-closed-doors chat with Mr. Garrett. He had quickly changed his mind. No one knew why and no one asked.

Suzanna Caldwell, longtime supervisor for the downtown studio had been demoted to simply manager when Edward brought Sheila Pickford back to Minneapolis after a dance seminar he attended in Kansas City. It was rumored that the young auburn haired Miss Pickford had been fired from her last studio, and Edward had been charmed enough to promise her the world. Women were his worst vice. Miss Pickford had proven to be a bit unprepared for her new position, and Suzanna had smoothed things over when need be. Sheila could ruffle a few feathers – both staff and students. Suzanna on the other hand with her delicate birdlike features and large owl glasses was an amazingly talented dancer as well as a generous human being who over and over settled many a volatile situation.

Today, neither Suzanna nor Sheila was on time. So when Edward's office door opened, and Larry Underhill accompanied Edward to the front desk, Mary Lou was standing there alone. Morgan had rounded the desk corner to the dance floor to play some music. The gleaming wide mouthed smiles of both men were almost blinding, and Mary Lou took a step back to gape.

Larry Underhill immediately introduced himself, slid her a business card and even gave her a charming wink of the eye. Mary Lou, normally immune to the attentions of the men in the studio, stepped back for a moment to take in this handsome man. Her frown turned to a look of enchantment and awe. Larry Underhill had taken her by surprise.

"Please, take my card and call me any time," he continued with 100% of his focus on Mary Lou. "And I really mean any time." His hand lingered on hers as she held the card. Then abruptly turning back to Edward Garrett he added, "I'll be in touch."

Edward smiled like a cat that just ate the mouse. His chipmunk cheeks puffed with his obvious pleasure in himself. Mary Lou didn't notice. Her eyes followed the back of Larry Underhill as he walked briskly out the door and onto the elevator to the top of the parking ramp.

Just at that moment when the elevator door closed, Sheila Pickford scampered in flinging her red hair away from her freckled face and breathing heavily. "Am I late?" She looked around at Edward and then Mary Lou with a surprised look on her face. It was not often she arrived after Edward Garrett. She brushed back her coat sleeve and squinted a look at her delicate gold watch. Then licking her lips she tried to hide her look of surprise and confusion. It was still early. What was happening here?

Suzanna emerged from the hallway. She must have been here earlier and squirreled away in the back office. Carrying her stack of reports, she nodded to Mary Lou and Sheila. She wore a navy and white print dress with handkerchief cut skirt that had become her "uniform" as of late. It was very fashionably current and the compliments she received when wearing the soft flowing fabric made it her dress of choice. She had on a pair of strappy black and rhinestone Latin dance shoes. With a square cut bobbed hairstyle and large round glasses, she looked like a delicate bird emerging from its nest.

"Antoine will be late. I spoke with him last night, and he had some type of morning conflict," she announced waiting for the cue to enter Edward Garrett's private office for the weekly meeting. Edward seemed excited to get started as if he were about to burst with some very important news. His chest puffed up and his wide grin seemed curious to the three executive staff members watching him bounce gleefully to the background music Morgan had put on. Music typically made Edward tap his foot or beat his fingertips on a nearby tabletop – he could be unconsciously be drawn in by background music.

Sheila, Suzanna and Mary Lou took the chairs around the large glistening cherry desk, and Edward leaned back into his comfortable desk chair before beginning the explanation for his unusually cheerful mood. "Today, we are on the brink of something new and exciting," he began. "We are venturing into the new age of advertising." The three waited breathlessly for him to continue. It took a few moments of him rocking back and forth before he added, "We are going to have a billboard advertising our studios."

"A billboard?" Suzanna questioned tilting her head as if she must be hearing incorrectly the words just spoken. "As in a roadway billboard? One of those hideous eyesores?" She grimaced.

"That is correct. We are going to have a huge, gigantic billboard right along the prime 494 strip. Everyone in the whole world drives the 494 strip and will see – us."

"Who exactly is 'us'?" Mary Lou questioned with a disturbed drag in her voice.

"Well, we will have to make a decision on that, now won't we?" he said tapping the top of his desk with his finger tips. Edward always tapped something – his fingers, his feet, his knees. It was another of his vices. Nervous tapping.

Sheila Pickford tossed back her mane of crimson hair and smiled brightly as if to say, "Surely he'll pick me to grace this billboard. I'm the obvious choice." Sheila was predictable without ever having to say a word. Her head tosses said it all. She sat with a lean back in her chair and her hands grasping the wooden arm rests. Her flower patterned synthetic clinging dress made her seem older than her twenty one years. She dressed like a seductive housewife who was trying to entice her neighbor's husband. She stretched out her legs and crossed them at the ankle then tossed her red curls once again.

Mary Lou Smith rolled her eyes just as Antoine Hawks flung open the door and with a ranting apology for being late grabbed a chair. "What did I miss?" he chattered looking quickly around at the intense faces.

"Billboards – the wave of the future. That's what you missed," Mary Lou droned her explanation.

"Billboards?" he stared with a puzzled look at Edward who still acted as if he just ate the canary.

"That's right. We are going to be featured on one of those huge advertising miracles right out on Highway 494," Edward announced again with a wave of his hand.

"Well, that will cost a pretty penny," Antoine whistled. Antoine Hawks was the new student counselor in the downtown studio. That means he made sure each new student was assigned a teacher matching their personality and dance needs. Then he would observe and make sure the lessons were going well. When it was time for the student to decide if dancing was something they wanted to continue with, he would assign a teacher from the advanced teaching department to continue with the instruction. His new student staff was specially trained to get the novice dancer started. It was a good system. In the suburban studio, Mary Lou did the job of both the new student counselor and the advanced department supervisor. She only had a staff of about five full time teachers to work with. The downtown studio trained any future teachers, so was a busy and populous place for teaching staff members.

"The cost will be offset by the results, I can assure you," Edward leaned forward beaming from ear to ear and lifting a tufted eyebrow.

"Well, if my results get any better, I'm going to need a bigger staff," Mary Lou demanded. "I'm at capacity for teaching time. We are booked up." She took her reports and slapped them down on the desk top. "Where are we going to get teachers who are fully trained with this short of notice?"

"I have that all taken care of, believe me." Edward smiled smugly. "It's going to work out beautifully."

"How is it going to work out beautifully?" Antoine leaned over the cherry desktop. His fashionable tie around the tuxedo collared dress shirt accented his sweet face – the kind a mother would love to kiss – soft, without the rugged unshaved look of a magazine model. He was lean and youthful with a spiky newly cut head of hair.

"I'm going to start a new training class from our students," Edward announced brightly.

"You are not going to take away my income!" Antoine defiantly replied. His income was based on the sale of lessons. And fewer students buying lessons meant less income.

"No. I'm going to take away _her_ income." Edward pointed to Sheila Pickford who looked startled and surprised. She had not yet figured out that her advanced department sales determined her paycheck. It didn't seem to dawn on her when she gleefully picked up her money every week exactly where the numbers came from.

"I'm going to take some of the advanced students and put them into a training class for both studios to use as teachers in their new student departments."

Edward once again looked pleased with himself. "We have a good group of young dancers who are fashionable and executive material. I think they will be flattered and excited to join our staff."

The rest of the meeting was a rousing shouting match between Edward Garrett and his executive staff. In the end, of course Edward's plan won – as always. After all, he was the owner. His schemes always upset everyone. That was the way his mind worked, and he seemed intent on keeping nerves raw and unsettled.

III.

The sign at the front desk was large and bold – "No Student/Teacher Fraternization". When dancing meant a ballroom full of retired ladies with blue hair piled on top of their heads, the sign didn't get much notice. But now with the popularity of disco and the median age of the studio students ranging from eighteen to twenty-five, that sign was given the once over by both students and teachers daily. Morgan Canfield cheerfully pointed out the sign to

16

any student who looked longingly at a teacher for too long. And lately each staff meeting made reference to the rule as the students coming in for lessons grew younger and more interesting socially. No longer the social reject who needed a few dance lessons to gain confidence, the new breed of student was not only confident and socially popular but good looking and with money to boot. The combination could be trouble for any dance studio owner.

The glass topped tables buffering the space between the wooden dance floor and the sunny windows were occupied early. A group of advanced students crowded together waiting for the daily group class beginning in fifteen minutes. Led by good friends Albert Rothchild and Cary Prang, the group met, danced and then went out to socialize each evening at one of the many popular downtown clubs. It was considered an honor to be asked to join the festivities of this group.

Cary Prang was a successful dark haired salesman always dressed in an executive looking suit and tie. His high energy movements and infectious laughter drew the attention of anyone who entered the ballroom. Even when he wasn't scheduled for a lesson, he would be at the studio looking to grab a partner for practice of some of his latest his latest steps. Newer students found this both intimidating and delightfully honorable. They would giggle and blush if chosen for a spin around the floor.

Albert was a year younger but just as dark haired and energetic as Cary. He was also a salesman but owned his own fledgling company that serviced businesses with the newly popular fish tanks. He was the one who had been commissioned by the owners of the new disco, Tara to develop their entryway. His latest topic to share with the group was the progress of this newest disco club to hit the cities.

"It is truly amazing," he was telling Kiki Mays, a University dance major who was taking ballroom lessons for college credit. "The dance floor is built right on top of the lower level bar. You can look down as you dance and see all the people seated below you through the glass floor."

"I'll bet that lower level will be a popular place to sit and look up the skirts of the dancers above," Kiki began to snicker at her own joke as she leaned closer toward Albert and squeezed his arm. Kiki was a beautiful woman in her early twenties originally from Jamaica. She had lived in the states so long that she didn't have any trace of an accent, but her father – a Jamaican diplomat from a small African country – had a sing-songy accent to his voice that was characteristic of the islands.

Sheldon Stein, another former high school friend of Cary and Albert's nodded his agreement. Sheldon was a new student just beginning lessons. Cary and Albert made a point to badger all of their friends to join them in the studio. "The more the merrier" was their motto. Sheldon was just as tall as the other two but his slight build made him appear smaller. Sheldon usually didn't say much, just nodding his short cut blond head when someone else made a comment. He was an only child from a well to do family who had never really had to work a day in his life. Laid back and easy going, his personality was quite a contrast to the energetic and boisterous Cary and Albert – two men who were driven in business as well as in their personal lives.

Also joining the group were Greta Rothe and her roly-poly friend Angie Cee. Greta was a highly unusual woman. Some say she was a private detective or working for the CIA but no one knew for sure. She had a mysterious sense about her that made the story seem believable. She would make an appearance each day dressed in the most unusual attire. One day it was a large wide brimmed canary yellow hat with matching yellow mini dress and matching yellow Minnie Mouse pumps. Another day it would be a tight black pair of 1950's stretch pants with high black turtle neck, black flats, a wispy black scarf wrapped around her head and neck, and sun glasses. She was totally unpredictable. Her teacher Carson Hunter always called the front desk before a lesson to check with Morgan on Greta's appearance and mood. Yes, her mood could be volatile. Some days she would come in laughing and giddy and other times she would cry through her entire lesson. She was a teacher's nightmare.

Her best friend Angie was round, blond and bubbly. To say the two were contrasting in temperament was an understatement. Somehow the two of them had wormed their way into this select group of dancers and managed to keep the gossip endlessly flowing. Maybe that was their contribution – somehow they always knew what was going on with everyone else. They had an inside line on each and every dance teacher.

"Want to know something interesting?" Greta sidled her back up to Albert looking the other way yet speaking as if she were a ventriloquist with a dummy on her lap. She hunched over and let a long strand of black greasy hair flop over her face.

Albert looked over his shoulder at the curled up back. Greta wore a loosely knit mohair sweater in hot pink and a pair of too short pants with large green window pane squares. She crossed her legs flicking a foot with a pointy pair of skinny heeled black shiny shoes with a pilgrim style rhinestone buckle across the toe. She made a quick nervous glance over her shoulder to see if she had his attention. Albert was staring at her or rather glaring at her.

"Well, do you want the news or not?" she questioned in a low voice at his obvious displeasure.

"What is it now?" Albert was not amused by the secretive way Greta had of getting someone's undivided attention.

"This is really good. I promise you." She glanced around to see if anyone else was paying attention. Cary was dragging Kiki to the floor for a Tango, and Sheldon had his eyes closed looking like a napping cat in the afternoon sun.

"You have my attention. Now spill it before I find someone to dance with," Albert snarled. He and Greta had had several run ins after he announced he was madly in love with his teacher Sydney Monroe. For some reason, Greta had not taken the news with the same humorous spirit the rest of the group had. She began to snip and make irritated comments whenever Miss Monroe was mentioned. It was a curious reaction to Albert's confessions of love.

"Ask me to dance and I'll tell you every detail," Greta said coyly.

"What? Oh, OK. Let's go." He grabbed her hand and yanked her up to the dance floor. Greta shriveled into a ball, wrapping her arms tightly around his neck and burying her head in his shoulder. He was only an inch or two taller than Greta, so the tight grip was snug. "Hey!" he pushed her away and started for the side of the dance floor as she reached out for his hand and gave him a sorry looking sad face.

"Get on with it, lady," he snipped as they once again got into a more proper dance position. "Well?" he prompted. "What is this news?" Albert's dance hold was stiff and tight, his back a bit too upright and his left hand holding Greta's always awkwardly pointing a few fingers out to nowhere.

"I heard that Edward Garrett is going to ask some of the advanced students to become teachers." Albert's head snapped back and a smile began to creep across his tanned face.

"Really? Who told you this bit of information?" he pried.

"My sources are confidential." Then she pulled away and walked off the floor. Turning briefly to look back at him, she added with a snappy crisp sound to her voice, "I told you it was good."

Albert stood in the middle of the floor looking like he had just won the lottery. Then he almost skipped off the floor humming to himself, his feet bowed out like a waddling duck.

IV.

When Antoine pulled Sydney Monroe into his office two years ago to tell her he had a student who insisted she become his teacher or he would quit his lessons, she had no idea what the implications of this news would have on her entire life. That insistent student was Albert Rothchild. He had come in with his fiancé to take a few lessons for their upcoming wedding. However, when he discovered shortly after the first lesson that his fiancé was also dating one of his neighbors, he abruptly called off the wedding. However, the dancing intrigued him. He wanted to continue but only if Sydney became his teacher. It was a rebound thing really. Immediately after the wedding was canceled, Sydney had been the teacher leading the first group lesson he took. He developed a crush on her – with her soft dark brown curls and engaging smile – she was the perfect person to take his mind off the failed wedding plans. It started off as just a winsome crush but soon he began to really feel something special for Miss Monroe.

She on the other hand took his attention as flattering but harmless. She pointed humorously to the "No Fraternization" sign at the end of each lesson. He was about five years younger than she was and certainly lived in an entirely different world. Even when the rumors of his crush reached her, she had to laugh at the absurdity of the whole thing. She had a steady relationship with a man for several years and that was something unusual in itself. Dance teachers tended to throw themselves into not only their dancing but also the whole work ethic, spending every waking hour in the studio with other dancers polishing and perfecting the craft of dance. Sydney was no exception to this. That left very little time to spend with someone who was not a dancer. It seemed to work, but the strains were often very evident. The nights when she would call and explain she just needed a few more hours of rehearsal time were becoming points of contention in the relationship.

Albert Rothchild was unique. He had a charming personality but was a bit volatile at times and could become very frustrated if he didn't get the steps right away. He felt a bit of a competition with fellow dancer and friend Cary Prang who had begun his lessons months before. They challenged each other in a good way but also could heat up the whole room when there was a bit of friction evident.

Today Albert had abruptly changed his mood from an angry growling bear to a singing flighty bee. Yes, he was practically on cloud nine humming and twitching unconsciously to the background music playing. When Kiki and Cary finally moved off the floor to rejoin the seated group, Albert was grinning and tapping his fingertips on the glass table top.

"How about Frankie's tonight?" Cary asked the group as he spun Kiki toward her vacant chair.

"Perfect. Sounds great to me," Albert chimed.

From the other corner of the dance floor, Edward Garrett was casually watching the student group chat. Edward was about six feet tall with a slender build and the expensive suit he wore looked model perfect. He glanced inadvertently at himself in the floor to ceiling mirrors that spread along the one wall of the studio. His curly hair was not his own. He wore a number of toupees in different stages of growth so it looked as if he had just had a hair cut or maybe needed one soon. Everyone knew about the hair piece, but Edward either didn't pay attention or chose not to listen to the snickering behind his back. He was now gazing at the group of young dancers seated around the tables at the other end of the floor. He twisted his mouth and pondered. He had watched the Tango Cary and Kiki had just finished and had also watched the strange display between Greta and Albert. With the music pounding, he had not heard the conversation but had merely watched the interaction between the dancers.

His eyes had followed the smooth and sultry flow of Kiki's flares and the interplay between the couple as they portrayed the dance of the Argentine gauchos. The Tango is done with both romantic playfulness between the couple and crisp violent struggles for power. Both Kiki and Cary played their parts with exact perfection. Kiki would flirt with Cary by seductively batting her eyes then just as the music changed to a more dramatic flair, she would pull away and try to avoid his gaze. Cary would pull her in and then push her away when she didn't respond to his advances. That was the dance of the Tango. Using the floor to step out long and flowing leg movements, the two of them moved from corner to corner like cats sneaking up on prey. Their technique was magnificent, and Edward smiled. His mind was working as he turned away to hide in his office for the remainder of the evening.

When the group lesson was over for the evening, Cary helped Kiki on with her sweater, a fashionable multicolored knit with a wrapping neck collar and chunky croqueted flower at the throat. Albert waved a few fingers at Sydney Monroe who was finishing a lesson, and Greta was being Greta – dramatic. She flung herself across the reception desk and pretended exhaustion. Morgan Canfield simply stared at her chewing slowly on a piece of gum.

"Miss Rothe, please!" Morgan knew Greta was looking with ferret quickness behind the desk for a new phone message or note on anything she could repeat to the rest of the group that evening. Morgan simply leaned forward over any writing that might be exposed to Greta's eager eyes. Greta lifted her nose in the air in a haughty pose and joined Angie in the corner. Angie was laughing loudly with a few of the older long time students who were sitting on the couches changing dance shoes to street shoes. Greta's mouth dipped at the corners and her black hair once again flopped over her angry eyes. After a few minutes of listening to Angie's conversation and shifting her mood back to normal, she glanced over toward the door to see Cary, Kiki, Albert and Sheldon already heading out the door.

"Come on," she snapped grabbing Angie's arm and dragging her toward the door to catch up to the group. Angie, round and powerfully built, flung the hand off her arm and sat down to finish changing her shoes. "Quickly, quickly," Greta prodded with growing agitation.

Frankie's was an art deco style building nestled among the downtown storefronts several blocks from the studio. The night air was fresh and cool. Occasionally passing a street person slung against the side of a building would bring mingling smells of oily grease and cigarette smoke. The group passed the glistening polished windows with elegantly dressed mannequins staring blankly out at the streets. The smooth modern metal contrasted with the sudden change in building style as they reached Frankie's. The brick and stone building featured stained glass windows and brass accents in an almost castle like appearance. Crowds were beginning to form around the heavy doors as people tried to squeeze into the dark disco. The dance floor was already packed with dancers and the rest of the crowds were pushing against each other to watch the slick movements of a few who stood out from the rest. A large glassy disco ball swirled above the floor sending chards of light around the room. Cary and Albert peered fervently around the room to find the best dance partners. Kiki was already snatched up by a tall slender dancer in sleek black pants and a black shirt opened down the front. Sheldon slowly ambled back toward one of the bars to grab a tall stool and order a drink. Greta and Angie scurried in and although surrounded by pushing people nursing tall colorful drinks with umbrellas and limes managed to slide past everyone to the spot where Cary and Albert were still scoping out the crowds.

"Albert, let's dance," Greta screamed over the loud music and chattering background conversations. Albert ignored her and continued his gaze. Greta grabbed his sleeve and gave it a tug. Albert looked sharply over his shoulder and pulled his arm back, his sweating forehead creasing into a scowl. Greta stood for a second then grabbed Angie and led her to the floor to dance. While dancing with another woman during the 50's and 60's was commonplace when the monkey and the twist were the dances of choice, the disco era with its partnered hustle was not so socially accepting of a woman dancing with another woman. Albert and Cary grimaced at the sight of Greta and

Angie doing some fast spins and even a sweetheart with Greta wrapping Angie up in her arms. The two women gave each other cutesy grins. The two men turned their heads as if to say "we don't know these people". Greta glared back in their direction.

The teachers from the studio would come shortly. Almost every night the staff would come out for a few dances before heading home. It usually took a while to finish up lessons and dance through routine practices before they showed up. But when they did, the floor cleared a bit to showcase their talents. Antoine Hawks pulsed his way to the dance floor with fellow teacher Megan Meeker. Antoine was a flashy dancer who always captured the attention of the audience with his charming smile and natural dance style. Megan was a jewel. She had short stylish hair that glistened in a purplish hue and her full lips were bright red. She wore a wrapped disco skirt in black with a black leotard underneath emphasizing her tiny waist and ample breasts. Her high stacked shoes had thick clear plastic heels and soles that allowed tiny lights to blink whenever she stepped on the floor. The crowds parted as Antoine and Megan took their spot in the center of the floor and began a smooth fast hustle featuring lots of spins and dips. Albert sighed. Oh, to dance like Antoine. That was

30

the thought of almost every pair of male eyes that stared at the couple. Antoine flashed a smile, and Megan ended in a long low dip to the floor.

Albert's heart began to beat as he recalled Greta's earlier bit of gossip. Was Edward Garrett really going to offer staff positions to some of the students? Would Edward think he could dance well enough for that honor? Would he be one of the chosen few? He would just have to make sure he was. He pursed his lips and grabbed Kiki for a slow dance. Carefully getting into his stiff upright dance position, Albert looked a bit out of place with the other couples wrapped around each other in more romantic clingy holds. Kiki chuckled a bit but let Albert lead her in a "proper" Rumba rather than adjusting his look to a more socially acceptable dance pose. He was a beginner – talented but someone who had not yet begun to interpret the music for his movement choices. That was an art Kiki had mastered well before joining the studio as a student. It's what made her look so natural as a dancer.

Greta on the other hand, once again to the shock of Cary Prang who stood defiantly on the edge of the floor, led Angie out to the floor for a romantic dance. Cary shook his head and looked away hoping no one would think the two women were with their group. He picked out a long legged blond in a slinky calf length dress of bright turquoise wrapped in colorful scarf belts. Then in spite of her awkward inability to dance many steps, he tried all of his new dance moves one after the other hoping she might pick up at least one of them. No such luck. She giggled in embarrassment and stalked off the dance floor as soon as the music ended. He would try again and again with other women, but to no avail. He asked Megan Meeker to dance and then tried to pry Kiki out of Albert's arms a few times. It was the usual evening at Frankie's.

V.

Once again the executive staff was squeezed into Edward's office. Edward spun nervously in his well padded desk chair swinging his lean legs around, then stopped to tap his finger tips on his glossy cherry desk top.

"The billboard shoot is scheduled for Tuesday morning. Eleven sharp. We'll meet over on 1st street in an upper warehouse photography studio. I'm meeting with Larry Underhill in a few minutes to finalize the details," he announced to the group.

He pondered a moment still drumming his fingertips in an annoying drone. "We'll have three couples,

I think. Myself and Amanda," he said referring to his ex-wife who usually partnered with him when doing dance shows. Amanda was one of the city's premiere models and always looked stunning. Tall and on the too thin side of slender, Amanda was not a "cute" girlish model but rather classic and elegant with dark brown curly hair piled on top of her head allowing a few wisps to frame her face. Her Roman nose was not the usual Nordic pug that was common in Minnesota. Although her lips were thin, she had the beauty of a Renaissance painting. Yes, the heads nodded in agreement. Amanda would be a logical choice.

Continuing, Edward leaned back in his chair as if deep in thought although everyone knew he had thought this through well in advance of his remarks today. "Sheila will partner with Daniel Loggerman." Sheila smiled coyly as if saying without any words, "Just as I thought". Daniel was a dancer who had joined Sheila in the studio after attending the dance seminar together. Sheila and Daniel were not what you would call friends – although no one was actually a friend to Sheila. So that part was not unusual. Actually the two had been roommates initially until Sheila finally became so disgusted with Daniel's irresponsible nature, she moved into a small efficiency apartment of her own. Daniel in spite of his casual and

33

sometimes annoying lifestyle, was tall, dark, and handsome. Yes, he would be a logical choice for the shoot as well. He had a look that would stop traffic - and that certainly was the purpose of the billboard.

It was most unusual for Edward to use first names and not refer to his staff as "Miss" or "Mr.". Today he chose to be more informal. "And for the third couple," Edward finally finished his train of thought, "I think we'll have Antoine and Mary Lou." Mary Lou made a loud gagging noise, clutched her heart and leaned forward as if to ask Edward to rethink this decision. Antoine leaned back and frowned slightly. Suzanna Caldwell, the manager of the downtown studio pressed her finger tips to her mouth as she always did when upset. Not that she had expected to be considered for the billboard, but to have Mary Lou chosen for the third woman in the shot was unsettling. Mary Lou didn't seem a logical choice in the least.

Mary Lou placed her hands firmly on the edge of the desk and glared at Edward. Most would expect this announcement to be an honor – a photograph that thousands of people would drive by and gawk at every day. But Mary Lou could only think about the humiliation in standing next to two young and slender women. People would laugh and point at the small chunky middle aged woman in the center. What could Edward be thinking?

She finally opened her mouth and asked the question everyone else was silently thinking. "Why would you put me on this billboard?" Her voice tone was crisp and demanding.

"You are the representative from the suburban studio. It is a perfect move to get your studio involved in the advertising," Edward smugly sat back in his chair.

"Why not take Charlotte or Becca or Jilli?" All three of the women teachers in the suburban studio were beauties. Each would be perfect for this billboard. Charlotte and Jilli with their model looks and Becca with her girl-next door innocence – they would all look lovely and certainly represent the suburban studio with elegance and style.

"Women don't identify with women who look like Charlotte or Jilli or Becca. But they do identify with you," Edward announced. Who had put this notion into Edward's little brain? This was not something that would normally come out of his mouth. Edward only saw beauty and model perfection when it came to appearances.

"And who gave you that little piece of advice? Was it Larry Underhill?" Mary Lou snarled.

"As a matter of fact, Larry did mention something like that. But of course, I agreed completely. So you will be our billboard model – like it or not." Edward's voice growled sharply and to the point. End of discussion.

A light rap on the door broke the mood momentarily. Larry Underhill entered and nodded to the group. His lapel flower was a white rose on a perfect black suit jacket.

"Speak of the devil…", Mary Lou glared at him and pointed to a free chair.

"Oh, I'll stand, thank you. I assume you are discussing the billboard shoot for next Tuesday. Great! Let's determine what you will be wearing," he stood in a comfortable upright posture with a smile that seemed to melt the heated fog that had emotionally filling the room just moments before.

"Sexy, sexy, sexy. That's what it should be," Edward beamed.

"Well, not exactly," Larry corrected with a cheerful lightness to his voice. "We want people to identify with all of you and not feel as if they are embarrassed to view the image over and over again. We want to draw them in as if to say 'this could be you. Can you imagine it?' So wear something colorful yet classic. That means a nice suit for the men with a casual opened neck shirt so it isn't too formal looking. Ladies, a nice dress, preferably long sleeved and to the middle of the calf would be a perfect choice. We want to appeal to the businesswomen and housewives who want to go for an occasional evening out. We don't want to appear as if we are from the local strip club, if you know what I mean." Larry was calm and collective as he described what he was looking for.

"Of course, that is perfect," Edward nodded in agreement as if that was exactly what he had meant to say – which of course, it wasn't. His chipmunk cheeks puffed in his usual pout when called to task on something.

Mary Lou softened. That sounded OK. It didn't seem too humiliating. Larry Underhill was certainly a very knowledgeable man. He knew what the masses would relate to. His charming smile and soothing voice tone had the entire room nodding in agreement.

"And hopefully, this campaign will fill up your studios so you'll have to add on dance floors – train more staff – make more money than you imagined possible." He spread his arms wide and pulled the group into his dream.

The nods and agreeable mood continued as the staff walked out of Edward's office and on to the rest of their day. Antoine pulled Suzanna aside and found a space along the hall to chat briefly.

"Sorry about the choice for the photo," he said as Suzanna waved away his apology as if to say "I could care less" which of course wasn't true. Then he continued. "I have a student who is ready to move into the Advanced Department."

"Why tell me? Why not let Sheila know?" Suzanna's impatience sounded this time in her voice. She was tired of covering for that empty headed novice.

"Because, I think I'd like you to teach this student yourself. It's Sheldon Stein. He's quiet and needs some kid gloves. He hangs with the advanced students like Cary Prang and Albert Rothchild. He needs someone who can create miracles, and you're about the only one I know who can do that." Antoine smiled his charming smile.

"Flattery will get you everywhere," Suzanna chuckled with a lighter tone to her voice. "I might consider it. When do you need to know?"

"Immediately. He is coming in at noon." Suzanna's response was a slight groan but Antoine knew he had her.

Larry Underhill was walking through the reception area chatting casually with Edward. "Mr. Garrett?" Morgan Canfield interrupted. "Miss Amanda on line one."

Edward excused himself, and Larry scanned the area for familiar faces to fill his next few minutes. Mary Lou Smith was getting ready to leave so he sidled over to give her a few words of encouragement. She felt a little bit of a flutter in her stomach as he spoke his upbeat "you can do this" words and held her hand briefly. Then she left, hurrying to make it back to the studio in time for the daily meeting.

Sprawled on the couch was a calm and surprisingly sophisticated Greta Rothe. She was drinking in all of the body language in the room as she crossed her legs. She stared at Larry Underhill and then cleared her throat so he would turn his head in her direction. Greta's black hair was pulled back into a sleek knot at the nape of her neck. She was wearing a little black dress with pearls around her neck and a pair of black pumps. She motioned with a finger for him to come over and join her on the couch.

Larry of course could not resist the attention. He walked over and stood in front of Greta as she once again uncrossed and crossed her legs again. He held out his hand

and introduced himself then handed her the usual card with his left hand.

"Greta Rothe," she returned with her eyes seductively fluttering. "I'm a student here. Are you a present student or future student?"

"I suppose I'm a future student," he smiled, his pearly teeth showing off a brilliant grin.

"Excellent," she nodded approvingly. "You'll love it here, I can guarantee that. Yes, I can."

Then Edward Garrett emerged from his office and motioned for Larry to join him. Larry gave Greta a slight tap to his forehead and lowered his chin for a brief salute.

Greta watched Larry walk off then peered around the corner of the reception desk to where Suzanna Caldwell was dancing with Sheldon Stein. The pair looked way too suited to each other. Sheldon's slender body was actually similar to Suzanna's, and he appeared inches taller. Greta smirked. "Now there's a couple," she predicted chatting to herself.

"Did you say something?" Morgan Canfield came around the corner carrying desk supplies.

"Nothing of importance," Greta returned a quick retort and settled back into her spot on the couch.

VI.

The photography studio was included in a block-long warehouse building that was square and uninviting. It was classic nondescript concrete with several floors of equally sized windows. It was hard to picture the studios inside as artistic and creative, yet that is just what they were. All of the studios in this particular building were occupied by artists and creative minds. The group filed into an equally gray entryway and elevator that opened to a dark but inviting expanse. The hazy and dimly lit room was large yet strangely cozy. Beyond the initial darkness was a softly lit space surrounded by large cameras and lighting equipment. The group dropped suit and duffle bags on overstuffed couches in the entry. Along one wall were partitioned makeup areas.

A shaggy haired man was adjusting his camera and seemed to take no notice of the group. Larry Underhill walked briskly into the studio and after nodding briefly to the models turned his attentions to the cameraman. Larry wore a pink carnation accenting his wide pin striped navy blue suit. He looked perfect as usual, and Antoine and Mary Lou commented how "in charge" Larry always appeared. Larry Underhill even had Edward Garrett agreeing with anything he said. That was someone who was truly in charge.

Edward was of course the last one to arrive, however, he was almost on time. Today he was a bundle of nervous energy. It was evident he was very involved and interested in this whole project. Was it the picture up above the speeding cars or was it the increased revenue generated by a new advertising plan? It was hard to tell with Edward. But he was certainly intrigued by the whole idea.

Amanda had flung her ankle length fur onto one of the couches and was busy helping the other women with their makeup and hair. Amanda knew fashion, and she knew what would look just right in front of a camera. Mary Lou looked classic in a yellow patterned dress with a green jacket, and Sheila was in blue with long gathered sleeves and a fitted waist. Amanda smiled approvingly and added touches of blush and appropriate lip color. She would squint getting almost nose to nose with her subject then take her head back to stare for a few seconds to evaluate before commenting "a smudge more of liner" or "smack you lips together."

Larry suggested Amanda take down her usual "disco tail" flopping on the side of her head. "We aren't really promoting disco but rather the dancing in general. We want this to be timeless," he explained as she undid the topknot and let her curly dark hair fall almost to her shoulders. He nodded his approval.

The shoot began with Edward complaining about the back drop used – a non-descript gray tone. "Edward, the beauty of this photo is there will be no background at all. The figures will be cut out so only this group will be visible on the billboard. The sky will be your backdrop. With no square or rectangle shapes to the ad, people will be drawn in even more," Larry explained holding up a drawing of the vision he had for the board. Edward nodded as he began to understand the concept for the photo. A grin began to cross his face as he joined the others in the center of the floor. Edward and Amanda were on the right with Antoine and Mary Lou on the left, and the taller Daniel with partner Sheila taking the center back. Each was in a dance hold with a slight dip or tilt to the side and overlapping to create an amazing group shot.

"I think this will work out nicely," Larry and the cameraman chatted as they both looked through the lens at the placement. And the shoot was on.

Edward was giddy with excitement and even offered to take the group out to lunch before heading back to the studio. Not that Edward Garrett was cheap, but taking a group this size to Carmelo's, the premier dining place in the downtown area was a bit extravagant. He ordered Escargot for everyone as an appetizer and asked for a bottle of Asti Spumonti.

Mary Lou found herself between Larry Underhill and Daniel Loggerman. She thought Daniel boring and self centered. So she turned her attentions to Larry who seemed just as attentive to her in return.

"So how many of these billboards do you do each year ...or month? I don't know anything about your business." Mary Lou smiled sweetly as Larry told her briefly about the advertising business. He was not one to complain or go into elaborate detail. He only emphasized the positive in everything he said, but seemed eager to talk one on one with Mary Lou. Was that something he did when speaking with everyone or was she really of interest to him? It was hard to tell.

When the escargot arrived at the table, Edward prodded the reluctant Sheila. "You haven't lived until you try escargot at Carmelo's. Have you ever had these before?" Edward grinned at Sheila as she stared at the shells.

Sheila's milky complexion with just a hint of freckles reddened. Then with a toss of her wavy red hair she commented in her heavy southern drawl, "What are these slimy things? No, I've never tried escargot. I don't think I want to either."

Edward laughed and insisted just one was a must. "Take the shell and sip it down," he instructed.

As the two of them bantered back and forth, Mary Lou calmly placed her hand over her wine glass as the steward began to pour the Asti Spumonti. "I've got to drive back to the studio after this lunch," she explained to Larry who was watching her with a curious look.

"I'd be happy to drive you back," he said placing his hand over his glass as well. "I'm going that way anyway. My office is out on the strip."

"Thanks but no," she smiled. "I can't leave my car downtown. But you can certainly stop into the studio for a free dance lesson if you'd like. You deserve an opportunity to try out the product you are advertising."

"I think I'll take you up on that offer if you'll be my teacher," Larry said slowly showing his pearly white teeth.

"Absolutely," Mary Lou grinned back.

As the billboard group was enjoying a very sumptuous and expensive meal at Carmelo's, Suzanna

Caldwell was also enjoying her lunch. But she was at a little café in St. Paul sipping tea and gazing across the table at a most unusual companion. At this moment she had no thoughts of regret for not being chosen for the billboard. She was actually quite pleased to be away from the shoot.

VII.

Edward Garrett didn't leave anything to chance. He already anticipated the added students the billboard was going to bring to both his studios. He sat in his office with Kiki Mays seated across the glossy wooden desk top staring at him as he spoke. "You have a dance major at the U so this would be the perfect opportunity for you. This is exactly the job you would want after you graduate anyway, so just start early by going into our training class and become a teacher early. It would save you time and money."

Edward's charming smile softened Kiki's expression. She had a beautiful face surrounded by a halo of kinky black curls. Her dark brown eyes looked past Edward to the ceiling as if she were deep in thought. It wasn't as if money meant nothing to her – her father was well off and her college expenses had been paid, but she was well aware of the necessity to have a career she enjoyed when school was over. She had always hoped it would be a dance career. Here was her chance. It meant more time, of course. She knew the training classes were held from six pm to ten pm every evening Monday through Friday. That was quite a commitment of time. But if it was something she loved, would that be such a sacrifice? Her thoughts spun around in her head. Edward's chatter just seemed to surround her without ever entering. She knew what he was saying without listening to the words – a hazy background echo in a thunder storm.

She crossed her legs allowing for her softly patterned skirt to drape around her calves. Her off the shoulder shawled sweater slipped a bit as she leaned forward placing her elbows on the desktop. She laced her fingers together and pressed two fingers to her lips. Slowly she replied, "I think … I would like that very much."

After a few more minutes of chatting, Kiki left the office to find Cary Prang. He was seated in the reception area listening to a tape recorder placed up to his ear. One leg was crossed over the other, and he paid no attention to the others coming in the door or going out. Cary always could lose himself in his own world as if everyone else rotated around him. He had his business suit on from a day's work as a salesman – gray with a gray and magenta artsy patterned tie. She waved to him and motioned for him to join her outside. Then they walked out to the plaza next door to the parking lot.

Kiki and Cary had already spoken of Edward's plan to invite some of the advanced students into the teacher training program, so it wasn't a surprise that Kiki had been approached by Edward. The two of them sat on the stone ledge that surrounded the plaza. Kiki told Cary of her invitation, and he nodded his head slowly. He would wait for his invitation. He knew Edward Garrett would approach him soon about the teachers' program. And he knew what his answer would be.

VIII.

Days later Cary and Kiki had begun their nights of training. It was tiring and exciting at the same time. They would dance for fifty minutes then take a ten minute break just like the full fledged teachers. This would be the schedule from six o'clock until the studio officially closed at ten.

48

Albert Rothchild sat glumly in the reception area. His sleek black hair stood up away from his face in a pompadour style with one strand of hair curling down over his forehead. He could see Kiki and Cary dancing around the corner of the room nearest to the mirrored wall. They seemed to laugh way too much, he thought. After the two of them had joined the teachers' evening class, he had abruptly made an appointment to see Edward Garrett. Where was his invitation? His eyes narrowed as he was lulled to thought by the music pounding out on the dance floor. His mind went over the different scenarios.

Greta ambled in and spotted Albert sitting stone faced on the reception couch. His eyes avoided hers as she moved closer. Greta had not received an invitation either. Initially she had shown her usual pouting anger at the omission but suddenly her mood changed. Suddenly her mind had clicked onto something that she chose not to share with anyone else, and she was almost pleasant. Someone should have asked what had changed her mind, but they didn't. Greta always seemed to gravitate to a new mood, so this pattern was not new.

"What's the matter, Albert?" Greta purred as she plopped down on her favorite couch.

Albert ignored her. She slid over on the couch next to him and began to put her hand on his knee. Usually Albert would angrily fling her hand aside, but today he didn't even seem to notice.

"Oh my, oh my," she shook her head slowly with wide eyes fluttering. "This is worse than I thought." She followed his gaze to the two dancers out on the floor doing a Cha Cha. Kiki was moving smoothly around the floor. Cary had a bit too high of a top line and looked a bit uncomfortable at the moment. But they were laughing. Sydney Monroe was teaching another student in the center of the floor, and Greta's own teacher Carson Hunter was twirling a tiny frail older woman. Daniel Loggerman was seated at one of the glass topped tables along the windowed wall with a stack of black folders.

"What's the matter? Want to dance?" Greta's soothing voice was anything but comforting.

"I have an appointment with Mr. Garrett," was Albert's short but crisp answer.

"What time are you meeting him?" Greta stroked his leg.

"Two hours ago," came back the angry reply.

"My, oh my," Greta's face began to curl up in a slow drawn out smile. Her eyes glinted with an evil flash.

Then she slowly rose and meandered out to the dance floor to pester Daniel. She licked her lips like a cat who just swallowed the bird.

Morgan Canfield sat behind the reception desk and occasionally stared over her reading glasses at the irritated Albert Rothchild. She had warned him as she warned everyone else who had an appointment with Edward. Edward would be late. But it never quite sunk in until reality and the long wait drove some of his appointments to finally leave. That may have been his motivation for being late – after all if you never hear about a problem situation, the problem situation just goes away. That was Edward Garrett's philosophy. Albert however was not going away. He would sit in that same spot and wait, sweat dripping down his forehead until Edward finally arrived.

As Edward made his usual grand entrance with a quick stop to greet Kiki and Cary, Albert rose with a determined look on his face. He was clearly trying to control his anger, but was not about to let Edward go into that office of his without him. He stood in the doorway and waited impatiently. Edward was trapped. He would be forced to meet with him. Edward stopped when he saw Albert, calmly checked his messages and then escorted Albert into his office. Morgan just shook her head and wondered how she had ever survived this job after the first week. A sane person would have run at the first sign of Edward Garrett's unusual personality. Was she that insane?

An hour later when Albert left the office, he was a new person. He was smiling and even did a few little Samba steps around the reception room. This made Morgan even more suspicious. No one ever left Edward's office in a cheerful mood. Immediately her intercom buzzed, and Edward's voice requested she come to his office. The visit was short and sweet. "When Miss Monroe is finished with her teaching this evening, please ask her to step into my office. Thank you."

Albert was nowhere to be seen when Morgan returned to the safety of her reception desk. But Greta was curiously circling the desk and no longer looking like the happy cat she had been an hour ago. Morgan quickly moved around the desk to protect any private notes Greta was about to pounce on and misinterpret. Greta was not easily distracted from her mission, but Morgan managed to shoo her away with a tart piercing look and a smart remark about her nosiness.

"Miss Monroe," he began when Sydney entered the forbidden sanctuary. She had never been into Edward's office directly – or indirectly for that matter. He had a few personal objects around the room. Some art pieces he had collected from his trips to the Caribbean were on the walls and a framed photo of a pair of young smiling children on the corner of his desk. Edward looked both pleased and disturbed. He smiled but it didn't reach up into his whole face.

"Sit down," he commanded. Usually quick to speak, this time he seemed to drag out his thoughts before saying anything at all. "I've just had a conversation with Mr. Rothchild. He very much wants to become a teacher in this studio."

Sydney Monroe inhaled deeply. This was not what she had expected nor wanted. Not only because he was one of her best performing students, but also because she knew he had deep feelings for her that so far she had been able to ignore. The student-teacher relationship rule had saved her from making any decisions about Mr. Rothchild at all. She could avoid any personal involvement with the man as long as he was a student and she was a teacher. She thought Edward Garrett was well aware of the rumors circulating through the studio about Albert's feelings for her. She knew he was aware, and her heart hardened in anticipation of his next sentence.

"I told Mr. Rothchild he needed a little more work before I could consider him as a teacher candidate," Edward revealed slowly.

Sydney smiled. So he did know, and he had made a decision that would protect her from Albert.

"However, I told him if he purchased a teacher training program for seven thousand dollars, you would teach him every day until he was ready to enter the program Mr. Prang and Miss Mays have started." Edward lowered his eyes and could no longer look Sydney in the face.

"What! You told him what?" Sydney repeated sharply. She couldn't believe her ears.

"Starting tomorrow you will be teaching Mr. Rothchild and only Mr. Rothchild. You will teach him eight hours a day and hopefully by the end of the month he will be ready to start the official teachers' program." Edward Garrett's voice was firm but had a bit of a waiver in it.

Sydney Monroe felt as if she was about to collapse. How could the man do something like this to her? Quickly he dismissed her with a wave of his hand. She felt numb. This month was going to be hell. Edward Garrett had bought and sold her. She felt like a piece of property. It wasn't as if she disliked Albert Rothchild, but at the end of this month she would either feel terrible that she had led him on and allowed him to spend his money for nothing, or she would have to be open to starting a relationship with the man out of guilt. Either way, it was disturbing. And the man responsible for this whole mess was Edward Garrett.

Sydney Monroe stalked angrily down the hall to the teachers' office to collect her belongings for her bus ride home. Tossing her dance shoes carelessly into the corner of her small allotted spot in the dark room they called the teachers' office, she quickly snapped up her bag and flung a sweater around her shoulders.

"Aren't you going to rehearse with me tonight?" Daniel snarled from his corner of the room.

"Sorry. Not tonight. I suddenly have a splitting headache." She flounced out with no further explanation.

Once home she dropped her bag inside the door and stared at Todd sitting on the ratty old couch pressed against the back living room wall. He was watching TV and grinned at her as she walked in.

"So how was the dance business tonight?" he asked with a sweet sincere swing to his voice. "You're home early." Then he patted the seat next to him inviting her to snuggle up and watch a late night talk show with him.

"Oh, it was great. Just great," Sydney answered back with stiffness in her tone. She looked at him – muscular, kind, always smiling, and so not interested in the studio. What was the addiction that kept her dancing? Why didn't she just marry Todd and live a normal life like everyone else? Normal and uncomplicated. A life where emotions weren't a part of each and every day. One where someone wasn't always pulling the strings. What kept her going back? She would have to talk with Suzanna in the morning and let her know the situation. Suzanna would understand.

IX.

Albert Rothchild stared at himself in the bathroom mirror. His handsome face was framed with a backward combed halo of black shiny hair. As a child Albert had been rather round and the target of ridicule from the other more athletic boys his age. So he had immersed himself in activities like music and theater. When he reached high school, he had slimmed down but his muscle tone remained flabby in spite of his outward appearance of health. He had become both bold and self reliant as his music talent propelled him into a professional career at an early age. By the age of sixteen when most boys got their drivers license and begged their parents to borrow the family car, Albert was driving a Cadillac he had paid for himself. Now this ballroom dancing was building muscle and popularity at the same time – something he hadn't experienced during his teen years. Today was going to be the start of a new life for Albert. He smiled knowingly into the mirror. Today he would begin the start of a much anticipated relationship with the woman of his dreams – Sydney Monroe. Once she got to know him on a different level – not just student/teacher – he knew she would be his. And Albert Rothchild had learned over his short lifetime never to take "no" as an answer. His chiseled face registered a new and delighted smile.

He walked out into the bare living room he had planned to share with his former fiancé – the one he had dumped when he discovered her affair with another man. The whole situation had taken its toll on Albert. He had immersed himself in his dancing and his new friendships rather than take the time to decorate his new house. It was empty, and it didn't bother him one bit. There would be plenty of time to make this homey when he was through with other things. His house was the last of his priorities at this time.

Across town Sydney Monroe was sitting down with Suzanna Caldwell for coffee before the start of the dance day. Usually she went in early to Edward's daily exercise sessions, but today she couldn't stomach the thought of spending a few hours with the annoying Eddie G knowing what he was about to do to her life. Instead she sipped a cup of hot coffee with a touch of cream and poured out her dilemma to Suzanna. Quite simply she felt Edward's recent deal with Albert to be a horrific burden on her personal life. Her stomach already was beginning to sour as she told her story.

Suzanna sat with her usual wise owl expression of calm and fingered her lips as she usually did when troubled. "I wouldn't worry about it at this time," she finally said with a smile that wasn't quite sincere.

Suzanna's mind was traveling to other thoughts. As she listened to Sydney her mind went back a few days when she had told Cary Prang they needed to stop seeing each other. She hadn't anticipated the new twist in the studio that had thrown Cary into the teachers' program immediately after she ended their short but torrid affair.

Now she was regretting everything she had said to him. But no matter. She couldn't undo what was already done. Yes, Edward Garrett had put a new kink into her life as well. She just wasn't at liberty to tell anyone about it. Sydney was talking future – Suzanna was thinking past. This was a new day and a new start for Suzanna.

Edward Garrett gathered up his new brood of teachers and his old faithful few in the center of the glistening wood floor. Sydney Monroe and her new pupil Albert Rothchild were in the corner learning steps. He called them over as well.

"You two might as well learn this while I'm teaching it," he growled then tried to sweeten his tone when he realized there were so many new faces staring at him. "I have developed a new disco dance that will be spotlighted throughout the country over the next few weeks. It's a slow disco dance based on the Fox Trot called the "Sway". Our studio must be top notch in dancing and teaching this new dance. We will be the experts!" His voice became firm and demanding.

Grabbing Megan Meeker who happened to be the closest female teacher, Edward began to take the movements of the Fox Trot and add subtle sways and dips that kept it firmly in one place on the floor rather than moving around as the Fox Trot naturally did. "It's the wave of the future and something disco needs. It's sexy and smooth and romantic... unlike any of the other fast and spinning disco dances we do now. Music is changing to incorporate some of the softer moods. We need to keep up with the trends."

Sheila Pickford sulked arms crossed on the side of the group staring at Edward dipping Megan Meeker again and again. She tossed her mane of hair back away from her face and pouted. Her mind was racing. Why hadn't Edward chosen her to showcase this new dance? Well, he'd hear a few choice words from her after this dance session was over. She wasn't about to take a back seat to any of these pathetic teachers. She lowered her chin and glared at the pair.

With lack luster excitement, the dancers took partners and began to follow along the steps and style of the new Sway dance. Sydney and Albert stayed on the perimeter of the group. Edward took some time to adjust and fix the mistakes he noticed in each couple. When he reached Sydney and Albert he took extra precautions to treat them with special attention. He knew he had played with fire and now he was wondering if he would regret it.

Albert was attempting the slow dip, lowering Sydney toward the floor. Then suddenly his upper body strength flinched, and Sydney landed with a thump. Albert's face turned a bright shade of red as Edward Garrett helped Sydney to her feet. Only a few of the teachers noticed as most were absorbed in their own problems with the steps. But Albert was indeed embarrassed by the move. Sydney turned toward him and smiled calmly.

"Believe it or not, that happens all the time in this business. Even the best go through a few falls before they master a step," she whispered.

Albert wiped the sweat that was beading on his forehead and grinned back. He took a deep breath and began to try the step again. It took about ten or eleven drops to the floor before he began to understand the position he needed to balance his partner's movement. It came slowly and when he finally felt comfortable with the pattern, it was a breakthrough. They walked off the floor with a renewed confidence. That was the moment he realized this decision to become a dance teacher was about more than "getting the girl". It was about challenging himself and finding new outlets for his creative yet stubborn streak. Yes, dancing was something that he needed right now.

It was just after lunch and the traffic was buzzing in all directions as Sheila Pickford sat in the older sedan next to Antoine Hawks. The tongue lashing Sheila vowed to give Edward Garrett was suddenly postponed when he casually mentioned the billboard was put up this morning. Antoine, Sheila, and Daniel had made a quick trip out to the highway to take a peek at the billboard. First, they drove by. Then they took the next exit winding around some of the side roads and frontage paths to find a clear view from across the highway. They stopped and stared at the larger than life square with their cut out figures rising from the top. Sheila's mane of red hair floated back from her face as she and Daniel in the back of the triangle of dancers smiled out to the passing motorists. Daniel looked tall and dark as he posed with Sheila. Antoine had a giggling schoolboy face as he held a tiny Mary Lou Smith leaning back to her right side with her look of laughing enjoyment. Edward had his usual chipmunk grin and Amanda looked tall and sleek as her dark eyes made contact with each driver on the road. It was quite impressive.

"Here, here," Sheila was prodding Antoine. "Take a picture." She handed him her camera and sucked in a breath of excitement. "They'll never believe this back home without proof positive." Her Southern drawl was heavier than usual.

Taking the afternoon off, the three had decided to swing by the billboard before stopping at the suburban studio for a quick chat with Mary Lou and the teachers there. As they walked into the loudly wallpapered waiting room, they were greeted by the receptionist behind the towering desk in the middle of the narrow reception area. This studio was not the subtle and subdued format of the downtown studio. Edward had taken the faddish silvers and bright colors of the disco era and created a striking studio that overwhelmed at first glance. The walls were patterned with loud and vibrant swirls. The carpet was geometric with a dizzy display of color and shapes. Sheila raised an eyebrow as she stared at the narrow entry with no windows. It seemed like a loud and busy barn.

Mary Lou was coming out of her office at the far end of the dance floor with a smiling Larry Underhill. She was laughing as she escorted him to the front desk.

"Good afternoon," he greeted as he stuck his hand out for a shake. "See the billboard?"

"Amazing," Antoine said as he pumped Larry's hand. Daniel and Sheila nodded quickly in agreement. Daniel pulled up to his full height and sucked in his stomach puffing out his chest. Sheila tossed her head of hair and combed her fingers through the curls.

"I'll have to go out and see it for myself," Mary Lou responded with a coy shrug of her shoulders. No longer hostile about the billboard, she was finding it surprisingly exciting to be seen by thousands of travelers.

"I'm here to learn a little dancing," Larry explained as he leaned on top of the reception desk to snatch up an appointment card. "I thought I might as well try out my own advertising."

"So we'll see you tomorrow," Mary Lou smiled and waved as Larry Underhill glanced at his card, nodded in agreement at the time selected, and walked out the front door. He took a moment to wave back at the cluster staring after him.

X.

Mary Lou had indeed enjoyed her first view of the billboard. She admired the tasteful yet colorful image of the dancers having a thoroughly enjoyable time. On her next lesson with Larry Underhill, she found herself gushing too much. He seemed to take the compliments in stride yet had a bit of a distant look to his normally vibrant expression.

Today Larry wore a pale gray suit with a crisp white shirt, yellow and gray flecked contemporary print tie and a yellow carnation in his lapel. Yet in spite of his initial excitement to begin his dance lessons, today he seemed brooding and preoccupied.

"Mr. Underhill," Mary Lou stopped him in mid step. "What seems to be bothering you today?"

"What? Oh, bothering me? Nothing … nothing really." He shook his head with a careless abandon, but the smile that usually spread across his face was gone.

With a bit more prodding, Mary Lou led him to a more private corner of the dance floor, and he began to unload a bit. It wasn't much, but Mary Lou soon pulled some of the reason for his unusual mood. Edward Garrett hadn't paid him for the billboard yet.

"I'm sure you'll get your money soon," Mary Lou smiled a hollow pasted on smile. In the back of her mind she began to think. Would Edward really do something like this? Would he skip out on paying Larry Underhill? Edward had a habit of spending more money than he made. He was a material kind of man who thought nothing of handing out a promise and having nothing to back it up.

Mary Lou tried not to look concerned, but she was worried about his blatant disregard for others. Money was another vice Edward Garrett had or rather didn't have. Edward never had enough money because he spent, spent, and spent more.

"I wouldn't normally be so worried about this, but that particular billboard was extremely expensive to produce. It cost quite a bit of money. Not something I am able to cover myself. And that is what I did. I put down my own money up front because Edward promised to reimburse me as soon as the billboard was up. I wanted to get it up as soon as possible, you see. Well, it's up and now he's avoiding me. I've called several times trying to reach him, but he never seems to be in the office."

"Well, he may be preoccupied with another project," Mary Lou tried to pull an explanation from the back of her mind. "He seemed to mention something about a record project."

"Ah, yes. The disco covers," Larry settled back into a more comfortable frame of mind. "He mentioned a local recording company had contacted him about doing some covers for their generic disco albums. It seems like a very lucrative project. He may be waiting for that to finalize before giving me my money." At this Larry nodded his head and smiled a content grin at Mary Lou.

"I'm sure that is what it is," Mary Lou cooed. "Shall we get back to our Waltz?"

But Larry Underhill was not content to sit back and wait. He made a decision to drop into the downtown studio the next morning to confront Edward Garrett personally. The ride down the elevator seemed longer than usual. Larry Underhill stepped out onto the ground level entry, his black glistening dress shoes sounded loudly on the concrete as he took a few long strides to the studio door. He gazed inadvertently at his reflection in the glass – the brown suit he wore with the peach rose in his lapel didn't quite seem to be his color. No matter. It was professional and sharp to a fault.

Morgan Canfield sat as usual at the front reception desk. Her reading glasses slid down her nose as she peered up to see who was entering when the tiny bell sounded. She couldn't help but smile as she pushed the frames up and shook her dishwater blond mop of hair. "Well, Mr. Underhill," she greeted. "What are you doing here today? Do you have an appointment with Mr. Garrett?"

"No, not exactly," Larry Underhill dragged out the ending of the word "no". "I was hoping I would catch him for a moment before the start of the day."

"Well, you can certainly take a seat. I'm sure he will be here any minute," she lied with a perfect smile on her face – part of her job she had long ago decided. And she had become way too good at it.

Larry sat down on the sofa in the reception area just as Greta Rothe lightly scampered in the door. With a quick toss of her head, she spotted Larry. A sleek black strand of hair draped over her right eye. She coyly sat on the other end of the couch and slyly slid over to sit next to him. In an elegant ladylike manner, she settled in and crossed her leg. Wearing a short green checked skirt with a matching green knit top, she wagged a slender pointed shoe up and down to the beat of the background music. Today she had a thick black liner coating her eyelids and a pair of false eyelashes that flopped up and down as she slowly glanced over toward Larry Underhill.

When her attempts to get his attention did not create a reaction, she cleared her throat and chimed, "Why, Mr. Underhill. Whatever are you doing here today?"

Larry Underhill had clearly been deep in thought. His startled look toward the woman seated next to him was surprising. "Oh, Miss Rothe," he began. "Sorry about that. I was thinking…just thinking."

"Well, isn't that nice," Greta grinned back. "It's nice to think sometimes. Yes, it is. Now just what were you thinking about, if I might ask?"

"Oh, nothing, really," Larry hesitated.

"Come, come Mr. Underhill. We both know that isn't so, now is it?"

Larry began to smile. In fact he began to laugh. "Shall we dance? I've only had a few lessons, but I can Waltz." He put out his hand and Greta instantly placed her hand into his as they stood and moved out to the empty dance floor. Somehow in those few minutes of swaying and dancing and laughing at nothing in particular Larry Underhill hinted to Greta Rothe that he was upset with Edward Garrett. Then he hinted that it was a money issue.

People began to come in to start their day – teachers and eventually students. Larry and Greta danced until they began to feel a bit uncomfortable. The teachers were standing along the sides of the wall waiting for the daily dance session to begin, so the two of them moved back to the reception area and then out the door for coffee. Edward Garrett never appeared.

Later in the afternoon, Edward entered through the kitchen door in the back of the ballroom. He passed the mirrors with his usual stop to adjust his toupee and gaze for a moment at his own reflection, then he turned the corner to the front desk for his messages. Morgan Canfield looked up over her glasses and mentioned Larry Underhill's visit. Edward sucked in a breath of air but seemed to ignore her words obviously relieved he missed Mr. Underhill.

"Miss Canfield, I want you to cancel all lessons this Friday until, oh say four o'clock in the afternoon. We are going to be doing a photo shoot for a series of disco album covers at Tara. I need every teacher and trainee to be at that shoot." He picked up a stack of messages and quickly flipped through them with a look of disinterest. "Friday. Clear it out. Got it?"

"Got it. And Mr. Underhill?"

"I'll worry about Mr. Underhill." Edward Garrett turned and entered the solitude of his office.

XI.

Tara was dark inside with the usual glistening disco ball made of bits of glass twirling above the clear dance floor. Music was pounding in the background, and the cameras were placed strategically around the floor. Dressed in bright jewel toned leotards and wrapped skirts, the women teachers sat around a table as Amanda and a woman in an ill fitted tweed jacket circled to check make-up. With a large fat make-up brush in hand, Amanda generously applied added coats of color to the cheeks and chin areas while the other woman dabbed on eye shadow with flecks of glitter. "More is better," they chimed in unison as they touched up with lip gloss.

Sydney Monroe in a red strapless tunic and tight red pants stood in the middle of the group with pursed lips. Her strappy gold Latin dance shoes made her only slightly shorter than her partner, Albert Rothchild. Albert wore a black suit with an open collared white dress shirt. Although he had been to Tara many times to oversee the installation of his mammoth fish tank in the entry, this opportunity to dance with the studio staff was giving him new perspective on the disco. He glanced around the room with an eager anticipation of an exciting day.

Edward had on a silky cream colored shirt unbuttoned down to the middle of his chest with several heavy gold chains hanging around his neck. His shiny brown pants were sleek and perfectly tapered over his creamy leather Italian pumps. Between pats to his curly hair, he was frantically directing people to the spots on the floor he wanted for a disco party shot.

Amanda would partner with him for the first cover. She wore a glittery bronze leotard with spaghetti straps and a lacy brown ankle length skirt wrapped around the waist with a satin disco bag. Her bronze shoes were a spider web of straps. Her impatient face quickly turned into an expression of pure pleasure and joy whenever the camera turned toward her. Then it reversed back to a look of frustration as soon as the lens switched to another face. She was an experienced model and today it showed.

The twirling disco ball created a rainbow of reflections across the dark dance floor as the music pounded and the couples twirled in their tiny designated spaces. "Smile people," Edward would yell periodically as he flashed a chipmunk grin back at the group dancing behind him.

"Ok, that one looks to be a rap," the camera man called out. "Let's get the next one in the front."

Quickly, Edward pulled Charlotte and Antoine into the front couple space and moved off to the side. Charlotte was a waif of a woman with slender legs, arms and hips but a generous bust line that seemed out of place with the rest of her tiny body. She wore one of her own creations – a pale pink sheath that wrapped around her neck and down the front then seemed to swirl around her waist and legs. Her hair looked like a fountain draped to the side of her head and as she lowered her chin and fawned with large brown eyes at the camera, she oozed with innocent appeal. Antoine had a head of soft curls and a slightly opened collared shirt with a loosely tied skinny tie. He stood behind Charlotte with an arm posed as if he were spinning her. She gazed into the camera coyly for the next shot.

Edward chose a few more couples to spotlight and barked out orders as he watched the process from the edge of the floor. Mary Lou sat in the back of the nightclub waiting for a chance to zero in on Edward regarding Larry Underhill. She waited patiently for the excitement to die down. When Edward finally signaled for the music to cut, she strolled up and gently tapped his elbow.

"The billboard looks wonderful," she began.

"How is the effect on our business? Do you notice more infos?" he asked as he quickly glanced back and forth for things he had missed.

"Oh, yes. There seem to be lots of calls coming in, and I'm asking our receptionists to ask if they had seen the

73

billboard before booking appointments," she nodded his back still to her.

"Great idea," he seemed to be taking in every movement except their conversation.

"I was wondering if the expense of the advertising has been taken care of already or if there are new goals we should be trying to reach to pay for it?" That seemed delicate enough, she thought.

"Already done," he said without so much as a hesitation.

"It's paid for then?" she stammered with a frown.

"Done. If I say it's done, then it's done," he hissed.

With that Edward stalked away to give last minute instructions to Amanda who was pulling on her heavy fur coat and snatching up some make-up carry cases. Sheila Pickford stomped toward him to demand an explanation for not selecting her as one of the front dancers, but when Edward spotted her weaving out of the pack of dancers he quickly grabbed Amanda and headed toward the door . "I'll just walk you to your car, my dear," he announced loudly as he gripped her arm and tugged.

"Interesting," thought Mary Lou. She felt a bit more content with his quick answer and began to gather up her staff to arrange rides back to the studio.

Tara was beginning to look dark. The DJ was gone, the doors were once again locked and the lights off until the after work rush would begin around four o'clock or so. Around three thirty, the assistant manager flipped on the lights and glanced at the wait schedule for the evening. The floor to ceiling fish tank glowed and shimmered as she gazed through the colorful schools of fish flitting by when she saw something strange. She circled the tank and stopped with a gaping mouth. There stretched across the dance floor was a body – a dead body. It was Edward Garrett lying face down. There was a pool of blood seeping out from under him in a dark glow as the lights from beneath the glass blocked floor caught the liquid. It was horrible. That is what she would describe to the police as they corded off the nightclub and searched Tara for any signs of what had happened.

Did she know who the deceased was? No. She had just gotten to work. The nightclub had been rented out for a photo shoot of some kind. She did know that. That was why she had come in so late. Normally she would be at work around two, but the shoot was to end around four. So she had planned accordingly. Yes, it was a surprise to come in to an empty place, but she had assumed they had wrapped up the shoot earlier than expected. No, she hadn't heard anything. They would check with the other establishments around for any unusual noises, but Tara was very sound proof – it had to be with the loud disco music they played all of the time. It was assumed any noise would be self contained and not noticeable to the other businesses.

The police detective was called over to view the position of the body and the floor. "Hmmm", he tapped his notebook and asked the photographer to be sure to record everything. It was certainly of "great interest" he said to the team on the scene. The assistant manager peered around from her seat to see what they were talking about, but the darkness and shadows from the lights blocked anything they were noticing. What hadn't she seen?

XII.

Morgan Canfield waited a moment after the ding of the bell to look up from her paperwork. She stopped and stared – two men - one in a dark trench coat and the other in a uniform. Certainly not your typical dance students.

"Yes?" she peered over her reading glasses. "May I help you?"

"Is this studio owned by a Mr. Edward Garrett?" the man said slowly looking at a notepad in his hand.

"Yes, but Mr. Garrett is not in at the moment. May I take a message?" She was cool and calm even when they flashed their badges. "What has he done this time?" popped into her head immediately. "I'm sure whatever Mr. Garrett has done, there is some logical explanation." Her tone was smooth and soothing. "How many times have I said this?" thought Morgan in disgust.

"I'm sorry to report that Mr. Garrett is, …well, he's dead." The first officer in the dark trench coat said quickly. His face tried to appear sympathetic. He creased his forehead and lightly shook his head.

Morgan took off her glasses and lifted her head to shake out her mop of hair. "Was it a car crash? Accidental fall? Was he drinking?"

"I'm afraid, no." The detective said with a curious tone to his voice. "Why would you ask that?"

"Oh, Edward Garrett is one who seems to get into those kind of situations. He has a few vices," Morgan explained. Then she waited for an answer. She began to stare at the officer intently waiting for further explanation.

"I'm afraid, Miss…"

"Miss Canfield. Morgan Canfield."

"I'm afraid, Miss Canfield, that Mr. Garrett was murdered." He waited for a response.

Morgan paled and pursed her lips before replacing her glasses. "I really think you should speak with Suzanna Caldwell. She's our manager."

"First, I'd like to speak with you. If I may," he said in a quieter, calming voice.

"I really think you should speak with Suzanna Caldwell," she repeated firmly and quickly circled the desk. "I'll get her." With a swifter movement than Morgan Canfield usually showed, she scurried down the hallway to the offices.

Suzanna Caldwell immediately appeared from down the hallway. Morgan had just blurted out a few choice words – "Edward Garrett" and "murdered" had been the two she could remember saying. Suzanna spotted the two men and stuck out her hand for an introduction. "Let's move out of the waiting area to my office," she quickly suggested.

Tucked back in what was formerly a small dance room – hard wood floor, floor to ceiling mirrors and tract lighting along the walls – Suzanna slid behind her desk and offered the men two chairs.

"Now please, explain to me what this is all about. We just left Edward at a downtown disco where we spent the day shooting a series of disco album covers. He seemed very much alive at that time." Suzanna leaned forward trying to glean any words of explanation.

"You say you were at a disco shooting some photos?" The detective who introduced himself as Officer Allen questioned as he opened his notebook.

Suzanna nodded and explained the whole staff had been at Tara until about two o'clock when the album shoot wrapped up. "We finished a bit earlier than we expected. I believe we had the place reserved until four. Yes, there were maybe twenty-five of us. It was the entire staff from both studios."

"Could you possibly give me the names of all those who were there?" Officer Allen seemed to glance at the other man as if some of the pieces were making more sense. Suzanna nodded and began to scribble on a piece of paper. When she had finished and handed over the list, Officer Allen continued. "Did Edward Garrett have any enemies that you can think of?"

"Enemies?" Suzanna frowned.

"Well, did anyone have a recent argument or problem with Mr. Garrett?" Officer Allen explained. He was a handsome but ordinary looking man – dark hair, dark eyes, lined face. His was a face you wouldn't notice in a crowd.

"Everyone. To answer your question, Edward was usually at war with just about everyone," that made Suzanna crack a slight smile as she emphasized the word again.

"Really? Everyone?"

"Edward was a man you could easily hate. I can guarantee you could go down that list and find at least one confrontation with each and every person on there." Suzanna leaned back in her chair and pressed her fingers to her lips as she always did when upset or thinking about a distressing situation. This was certainly a distressing situation – Edward Garrett dead? Murdered?

"So, for example," Officer Allen slid his finger down the list. "Amanda Garrett."

"Ex-wife."

"Enough said," he agreed. "You?"

"He cut my income by hiring a new and unqualified person to take over one of my departments." She leaned forward and stared him in the eyes. "Money and humiliation. No better motive than that. However, I didn't do it – in whatever way it was done. You haven't mentioned that yet." She waited for a response.

He smiled. "No, I haven't, have I?" There was a moment of silence.

"So if his genitalia were mutilated, you could take my name off of your list," she answered back smugly implying her motive wouldn't have been sexual.

"No such luck. You're still on the list." He laughed and continued to look down at the names. Quickly he stopped at one name and leaning over to the uniformed man pointed at the paper. They both nodded. Suddenly, they seemed the conversation would end. "Well, I think we've taken up more than enough of your time. Is there a way we could interview some of these people on the list?"

"Most are here in the ballroom training or teaching. There are a few who teach at the suburban studio. I could star those names for you if you would like?" she reached for the paper and began to note the teachers from the other studio.

"Thank you," Officer Allen rose, quickly snatched the list back, and shook her hand. She accompanied him to the ballroom. Motioning him to wait at the desk, she gathered the group of teachers together and explained the presence of the officers. There was a gasp and low mumbles as they all took seats at the tables scattered along the windowed wall.

"They are ready for you to interview them. All except Amanda Garrett, of course. She isn't really a teacher, just Edward's ex-wife and dance partner. She might be at home or possibly working. She's a model," Suzanna explained to the two men and waved her hand to motion them into the ballroom.

One by one each teacher was escorted to Suzanna's small office. The others sat nervously mumbling back and forth to each other waiting for their turn. "What could have happened?" "How did Mr. Garrett die?" "Did anyone know anything about this?"

As each returned to the ballroom, there was no more information to share with the others. The officers had only asked questions but hadn't divulged any information to take back. As the group whittled down to only a few left to interview, the newest training class was at the end of the list and the final ones to be chaperoned into the interview room. Albert Rothchild was the final person, and he was technically not yet a staff member as he was still taking lessons during the day. He had felt a surge of excitement earlier in the day as he was included in the photo shoot. Currently, however, he wasn't feeling so lucky to be a part of this elite group. Especially when the officers instead of taking him into the room informed him he would be accompanying them to the police station. His face showed shock at first and then it turned to anger.

"What is the meaning of this?" he argued hotly as they placed his hands behind his back and cuffed his wrists. "I demand an explanation," he bellowed as they led him out the door. Cary Prang immediately sprang to his feet and raced for the phone at the reception desk to call a lawyer.

"Get down to the station immediately," he hissed into the phone. Then after placing the phone back into the cradle, he turned to Kiki who had followed him to the reception area. "My cousin," he explained. "He'll find out what this is all about. Never expected something like this."

The rest of the afternoon and evening was tense. No one seemed in the mood to dance although the music was playing loudly as usual. Cary and Kiki stood in the corner of the floor for the most part starting to practice a few patterns and then stopping in frustration as they thought about their friend whisked away to the police station for whatever reason.

"Mr. Prang?" Morgan Canfield called to him from around the corner. She motioned him toward her and held up the phone. "For you," she explained. Normally she wouldn't interrupt during the dance hour. A message could be picked up during the break, but tonight was certainly not a "normal" evening. She felt any message might be worthwhile and indeed this one was.

Cary listened carefully to the voice on the other end of the phone and then motioned for Morgan to get Sydney Monroe to the phone as quickly as possible. Sydney was just finishing up a lesson and walking her student to the front desk. She seemed unusually preoccupied all day. The departure of her student Mr. Rothchild had been more troubling than she could ever imagine. Why had Albert been taken away? She had racked her brain for an explanation and could find none.

"Excuse me, Miss Monroe," Morgan pulled her away from her student. "Mr. Prang needs you to take the phone as quickly as possible."

Sydney's face flushed pale as she scurried to the outstretched phone Cary was holding out to her.

"Yes. Yes. That is correct. Yes. I was with him until the officers showed up at the studio. Yes, that is correct." She answered question after question with short crisp answers and then hung up the phone quickly.

Turning to KiKi and Cary she explained in a low voice. "Albert told the officers that I rode back from Tara

84

with him after the photo shoot and was with him afterwards until the officers came to the studio to announce Edward's death. And although I know it is against the rules to fraternize with the students – and Albert is technically still a student – I did ride with him and spent the entire time afterward in a dance lesson. For some reason they suspected Albert killed Edward. But that is just not possible, and I am his alibi." Her face twisted into a worried look that almost appeared to be the start of tears. But she bit her lip and held back any more emotion.

Morgan sat back in her comfortable desk chair and mulled the conversation. What would make the police think Albert Rothchild to be guilty of murder? It just didn't add up. Not with what she observed around the studio. Albert and Edward didn't seem to be at odds, and although Albert sometimes showed signs of a temper, it didn't seem to be directed at Edward Garrett. In fact, he seemed to admire the man. Sometimes they almost seemed to have too much in common personality-wise. Both were stubborn and aggressive and certainly men who were driven toward their destination. They both seemed to admire those traits in each other. It was a mystery to be sure.

An hour or so later, Albert Rothchild walked into the studio with another man. Another dark trench coat. This time it was Cary Prang's cousin, the lawyer accompanying Albert. Cary rushed to the reception area for a briefing with the two men and nodding to his cousin shook his hand, thanked him, and sent him on his way.

Albert looked harried. He didn't have the usual sparkle in his dark eyes and his smile was no longer evident. He did seem to be relieved, but shook his head in frustration when Cary asked why he had been detained. Obviously there had been no explanation from the police as to this sudden move to suspect Albert. Sydney spotted them and scurried out to give Albert a big hug. As she began her barrage of questions, he simply shook his head and shrugged his shoulders. He had no explanation at all. They had some evidence at the crime scene that was connected to him, but no explanation other than that had been given during the ordeal. It remained a mystery to all although everyone seemed to be wracking their brains for some sort of clue to the puzzle.

XIII.

The local newspaper ran the story of the murder without the name of Edward Garrett mentioned. It claimed

86

the notification of next of kin prevented them from identifying the victim. The story said a body was found shot on the dance floor of the popular nightclub known as Tara. It did mention the time of day to be mid-afternoon and claimed there was no suspect or motive at this time. Very generic.

The teaching staff in the suburban studio had been interviewed with no more information filtered in their direction. Certainly the police were being very closed mouthed about any and all suspects and details of the murder other than to mention Edward had been shot.

Amanda had also been escorted to the police station, but with the shocking news of her ex-husband's murder seemingly to be the only reason for the meeting. They wanted to see her reaction first hand. That apparently was the only explanation. She was truly shocked and in spite of her cool and collected manner normally had broken down sobbing when told. She called her father and asked him to take her home from the station. It took her a day of sitting alone at home without taking phone calls before she realized she would have to be the one to plan Edward's funeral. Although technically not a blood relative, she was really his only next of kin within a reasonable distance. The dreadful task would fall on her shoulders. They wouldn't be releasing the body until a complete autopsy had been performed, so she would have to wait to find out how long that would take before she would set a date. The wait would be difficult.

Cary, Kiki, Sydney and Albert sat around the glass topped table in the ballroom and began to throw out an explanation – not just for the police detaining Albert, but for the murder itself. Who would do something like this? And more importantly, why? If they could just figure out the why, maybe they would be able to explain how this whole event had happened. It was apparent they would have to find the killer or Albert would be forever connected to this murder.

Sydney Monroe had been shaken by the whole situation. As she stared at Albert Rothchild's face, she began to turn over thoughts in her mind that had been previously so deep they hadn't surfaced before. Those thoughts began to trouble her. Why was she drawn to this man? What had made her so frantic when Albert had been whisked away by the police? Why had she felt so emotional? It was too complicated to explain. This man was so very different than she was. He was not only younger by about five years, but had lived a very different life than she had. They had nothing but the dancing – and

Edward Garrett's murder – in common. Yet she felt such emotion. It was frightening.

Albert was saying, "There was something at Tara that convinced the police I was guilty. We have to find out what that was otherwise we have nothing to go by. How can we find that link?"

Cary and Kiki nodded and stared into space. Finally Cary spoke. "We are going to have to find the person who found the body. That's all we can do."

"Let's try the staff at Tara. I know most of those people," Albert continued. "The fish tank at the entrance. I service it every week. I think someone there must know something."

"I could come with you the next time you service the tank and speak with the wait staff," Kiki offered. The two men stared at her. She smiled and explained, "They'll feel more like talking with another woman. Most are women I'm assuming." She gazed from one face to the other as they both nodded. "Yes then?" she asked.

It was agreed that Albert and Kiki would go to Tara tomorrow as scheduled to service the tank. Kiki would begin a conversation with the manager on duty as well as the wait staff. It would be during the day when the place was quiet and free of customers. Hopefully they would discover something of interest.

Conversation over, the two couples began to dance. Sydney praised Albert for his progress. "Your dancing has really improved so very quickly. I think you may be almost ready to take your teacher's test. Mr. Garrett said you had to be able to pass your full Bronze and into a good portion of your Silver program before you could officially go into the teacher's training program."

"What does the teacher's program do that we aren't already doing?" Albert was one who questioned everything. He always pushed the point, never assuming anything.

Sydney explained that while they were working in his lessons on dance technique, the teacher's program included methods of teaching. Good dancers were not necessarily good teachers. To do was one thing, but to impart that knowledge to others was entirely different. The teaching part was a gift. She didn't say so, but she silently wondered if the impatient and sometimes temperamental Albert Rothchild would actually be a good teacher. He was an asset as a student because other dancers could see his drive and determination as well as his quick progress, but for him to show patience with someone else who was struggling with a dance concept remained to be seen. Could he easily impart that knowledge to others?

Albert Rothchild was one who was extremely driven. He had realized at an early age that he had a musical talent and had focused on making money in the music industry from a relatively young age. He hadn't been the typical teenager with an active social life centering on high school activities like football games and proms. Instead he had spent his weekends and even weekday evenings playing music at clubs and social gatherings attended by adults. He had grown up quickly and had been sparked by the large amounts of money he was making from this lifestyle. He just as quickly spent the money he made. That was why Albert hadn't seemed very concerned with the expensive dance program Edward had suggested. As long as it got him to his end goal, the money hadn't been a concern. Did he have that large amount of money? Of course not. Albert was driven by the idea that he needed to spend the money first in order to make the money. Money clearly drove Albert to the decisions he made – it was what made him successful in his business. Spend it, then make it was his rule. It had been Edward's rule as well. Spend the money then make it to pay off the debt. So much alike.

The next morning Albert picked up Kiki from her campus apartment and headed for Tara. It was a dreary, cloudy day. At first the drive was quiet, but soon they were throwing out ideas on Kiki's approach. What did she need to ask? And who should she ask?

"Find out who found the body," Albert was saying as they found a parking spot. "We really need to find that out right away." Kiki nodded and scurried behind the quick walking Albert. He carried his bright blue bucket of supplies to clean the tank and waddled in without so much as a blink of an eye from the crew already beginning the day's set up.

Albert began the mundane task of chemicals and cleaning turning his back to Kiki. Let her do the talking, he told himself. Trust her.

Kiki lounged in the reception area and began to pick up conversations with the staff as they passed through. She had an easy going style that made people want to spill their life story as she smiled and nodded. The murder was something that could create a natural conversation.

"I just can't believe he was murdered here," Kiki was saying as she shook her head in apparent sorrow to the woman standing at the hosting podium. "We were here all morning and didn't see anything at all."

"Yes, it was shocking. I was the one who found him...".

Bingo! Albert tuned out the conversation and smiled. Kiki was doing her job. He was hoping she would find the key. The murmuring behind him was muffled by the sound of sloshing water. He hummed a quick little tune and bopped his head to the music he let swirl in his head.

"Ok, here is the story," Kiki trotted beside Albert back to the car. She was beaming as she pulled her wool coat collar closer around her neck. Minnesota winters were still difficult for the Caribbean native to adjust to. It wasn't a cold day, but she still felt the chill as she walked in the crisp wind.

Albert put his work bucket into the trunk and waited for her to continue. "At first she only noticed the body lying on the glass dance floor. That's where he was found – on the dance floor. That was shocking enough. But when the police came, they were taking pictures of something on the floor. She didn't get a good look at it, but it looked like something was written in blood on the glass tiles."

Albert frowned. "Something written on the floor? What could it be? What was written?"

"She didn't know, but the police were taking special interest in whatever it was. Of course, by the time the body was moved, everything had been cleaned off the floor. That seems to be the key. Something written on the dance floor." Kiki seemed proud of her discovery, yet it still posed the question 'what was written on the floor?' Only the police would have that answer. The Tara staff had been kept away from the crime scene after the initial discovery. They had reached the end of any more information from that angle. What next?

XIV.

Mary Lou Smith sat across from Larry Underhill sipping a cup of hot tea. She smiled sweetly and thanked him for the breakfast invitation. He looked as handsome as ever with a black three piece suit, silver gray tie splashed with dots of magenta and a white carnation in his buttonhole. His neatly trimmed mustache and smooth skin showcased his pearly white grin.

"This whole murder thing has totally taken its toll on my staff," Mary Lou peered over her teacup at Larry as she admired his calm and businesslike attitude. He was always the same – never so much as showing any other side than professional. It had been a pleasant surprise when he had invited her to a quiet breakfast at a local popular café. Certainly, no one would see them here together. Although with Edward Garrett gone, who would really care? That had been her rational through the whole debate she had with herself as she graciously accepted the invitation. After all, was he really a student or a business colleague? She thoroughly understood the concept of the "no student-teacher fraternization" rule. But was it actually the case in this situation? She had to agree it was borderline.

Larry smiled and then chuckled. "I suppose I won't get paid now."

"Oh, Larry. Edward told me at the photo shoot that the payment had been taken care of," Mary Lou gently put her tea cup back on the table and gazed at him with a troubled stare as he shook his head. There was an awkward silence then she added, "Don't you worry now. We'll get you your money. You can count on that. Suzanna and I will be meeting sometime this week as usual and will discuss the terms. Just give me your agreement, and I can assure you we will take care of this. Just because Edward is…deceased doesn't mean the business is dead. We are all going forward without him. It's business as usual."

"I was hoping you would say that," Larry leaned down and from his perfect business attaché pulled out a bill that he placed carefully in front of Mary Lou.

At first, Mary Lou leaned back. It was initially shock at the amount displayed on the invoice. But it was also a sudden pang of the deceit she felt. This breakfast invitation hadn't been social at all. It had been all business. And why had she expected it to be any different? Larry Underhill had never shown anything but a professional side. Wasn't that the same as in her own business – the dance business? She could just as easily say her staff showed nothing but a professional attitude toward their students, yet the students were constantly misinterpreting the gestures as personal attention with the intent of something much more. It was something she as a manager dealt with daily and here she was falling into her own trap. She felt like such a fool. Quickly she snapped up the invoice and threw it into her purse. Then she smiled back – a fake and hurt smile. Larry Underhill never noticed. He continued on with a meaningless conversation about billboards and dancing and everything else in the world except what she wanted to hear. Her foot began to tap nervously. It was an old Edward Garrett habit that had suddenly passed its way to her. How inconvenient.

Suzanna Caldwell was also enjoying a breakfast meeting. This one however, was in a quiet St. Paul nook far from the clatter of the downtown Minneapolis dance studio. Suzanna's breakfast would take a slightly different turn than Mary Lou's.

Sheldon Stein sat quietly picking at his mound of scrambled eggs. Sheldon was painfully thin and pale with a shock of blond hair. He seldom smiled as Larry Underhill did. But this quiet man held Suzanna's attention in much the same way Larry Underhill did Mary Lou's. Their dance partnership as teacher/student had evolved to something more than the professional. Suzanna surprisingly felt quite at ease with Sheldon just as he seemed to be with her.

"Should I stop by your place after the studio closes tonight?" he asked looking up calmly from his meal.

"Park around the corner so no one notices," she responded.

"And I'll watch the door for any studio people before I go in. Maybe I'll just let myself in before the studio closes to make sure."

"Make sure Amanda doesn't spot you," Suzanna added thinking about Edward's ex-wife who lived in the same four-plex.

Sheldon nodded and pushed his plate away. "See you then."

Sydney Monroe stood at the door of the two story house she shared with Todd and his cousin Rudy. The bareness of the furnishings emphasized the stark white newly painted walls and the gleaming polished wooden floor. How ironic. This floor was such a beautiful dance floor yet Todd showed no interest in dancing. Yes, he tolerated Sydney's intense interest in not only the dancing but her job at the studio. He tolerated and rarely said anything about her many hours and late nights spent with other dancers because he knew how happy this made her, but his life was so very different from a dancer's. His toned athletic body was sculpted by hours of working construction as well as the weights he kept stacked in the dining room off the old fashioned kitchen. He was just getting back from his daily run. Wearing only shorts and t-shirt even on this cool almost winter day, his muscled body was glistening with sweat. A sweat band wrapped around his head held his growing out mousy blond hair off his forehead. The crisp short hair cut he had had in the army was something he wanted to change as a way of eradicating that life forever. She knew he would let it grow to his shoulders in spite of the teasing he would have to endure at the construction site from the other workers.

Todd was not a typical laborer. He was smart as well as skilled. And most importantly, he had a heart of gold and a sweet spirit that made that silent smile seem so very sincere. It was unfortunate that the only thing Todd and Sydney didn't have in common was the one thing that was most important to Sydney – her dancing. He separated himself as much as possible from even asking anything about the studio and dancing. It seemed he wanted that to be her own secret life. That was becoming a problem for Sydney. She wondered where this all would lead.

Todd wiped his face with a small towel and gave her a kiss as she turned to leave to catch the bus for downtown. He smiled but his eyes were distant as if he wondered the same things that Sydney did about the relationship. His silence seemed to be the one thing that kept the relationship going, and he wasn't going to give in to the temptation to voice any disapproval. He couldn't bear to be the one who initiated the end of something he obviously felt was important to him. He was hoping Sydney's passion for dancing would suddenly wear off and their relationship would be back to normal again. Patience was one of Todd's most endearing traits. He would wait.

The ride down to the studio was quick but boring. This time of morning left the buses almost empty. The morning rush had long gone. And now that Edward's early morning dance and exercise sessions were no more, getting to the studio before noon was unnecessary. Sydney sat back in her seat and stared out the window. She felt anxious without knowing why. Obviously, Edward's death was something to make everyone feel uncomfortable. But this was something different. This was about life and not about death.

Albert Rothchild ran in for his lesson, late as usual. He quickly changed into his dance shoes and scurried out to the dance floor. It was early with no one else yet in for a lesson. The wave of dancers and practice times had changed since Edward's death. It was difficult to anticipate when anyone else would be out on the floor. The only thing they could count on was the time in the evening from six until ten o'clock. The floor was always filled with dancers each evening. Most students were working professionals with business conducted during the day and pleasures such as dance lessons saved for the evening.

Sydney put on a slow Waltz, and the two of them glided across the floor unhampered by other dancers taking up space. This was a luxury - a Waltz with no one to prevent the movement from continuous motion around the floor. Sydney gazed at the mirror in silent thought. She smiled.

"So what are you doing for the holidays?" Albert asked.

"What? You mean Christmas?" Sydney hesitated. Albert was Jewish, and she didn't really know if he was referring to the Christian holiday or something else.

"Of course I mean Christmas," he sounded slightly offended.

"We don't really get much time off here at the studio. Only Christmas Eve and Christmas Day. This is the time of year when everyone is getting ready to dance for holiday parties and New Year's Eve. So it's rather busy in the dance business." Sydney stopped speaking and kept dancing.

"So what are you doing for the holiday?" Albert was persistent with his original question.

"My parents live in a little town outside of the cities. So I will go out there for a few days, I suppose."

She answered his question with as little explanation as possible.

Albert's attention remained trained on his question. "And where would that be?"

"Chaska." Sydney hesitated only for a moment. What harm could it do to simply answer his question with an honest answer?

"I think I may be servicing a fish tank in Chaska that day," Albert retorted.

"On Christmas?" Sydney stopped dancing and stared into space. Now she regretted her answer. She should have been vague and generic in her answer.

"Of course on Christmas. Fish don't know what day it is," Albert laughed. "I thought I might just stop in to see you while I was in town."

Sydney began to breathe heavily. "I'll let you know. Keep dancing." Here it was the moment of truth just as she dreaded.

And the subject was dropped as they started a lesson on twinkles and spiral techniques. Sydney adjusted Albert's posture and reminded him of the topline sway needed to lead both patterns.

At ten o'clock when the day was over and Albert Rothchild was changing his shoes, Sydney Monroe appeared. Casually standing in front of Albert and with a quick glance around the room to make sure everyone else was preoccupied with other things, Sydney nodded. "The answer is yes." Then she walked away just as quickly as she had appeared.

"The answer is yes," Albert repeated with a sly smile. "The answer is yes."

XV.

Sydney threw her overnight bag on the floor of the entryway and shrugged out of her black wool pea coat. There was packed snow on the ground but no fluttering flakes to make the Christmas travel treacherous. The drive had been smooth and uneventful. Her dirty gold Demon was parked in front of the older two story house with the traditional front porch nestled next to the corner church. Her father, the pastor of that church, was listed on the sign just below the title of his Christmas sermon, "Silent night, Holy night".

It had been years since Sydney lived at home with her parents. Her younger siblings were also away at school, so this reunion would be special. Seeing everyone again was something she anticipated with excitement. She would have the questions, of course, about Edward's murder. Not that any of them knew Edward, but the news would have spread from one family member to the other. "Did you hear about Sydney's boss...", and so forth. There would be a million questions. She sucked in a breath of air and prepared.

"Sydney!" her mother greeted. "You look wonderful." Her mother held her at arms length to take a quick overview before giving her a hug.

Her mother was one who somehow could drag out the most hidden secrets without even asking a question. Her kind eyes and gentle smile gave most a trusting and instant connection. Sydney immediately followed her mother into the warmth of the large country style kitchen to fill her in on all the latest details of her busy life while mom baked – finishing a batch of cookies by spooning the sweet mixture onto a flat sheet. Sydney's mother was always baking something. It was something she missed in her own home in Minneapolis. There were never any sweet treats in her own stark kitchen. With health enthusiasts Todd and Rudy living in the house, it was more common to find a bag of natural granola rather than a filled cookie jar.

As her mother nodded patiently after popping the sheet into the oven and turned her attention to stirring a bubbling pot of homemade peanut brittle, Sydney poured out every detail. Perched on a stool and breathing in the sugary aroma of the candy mixed with the pine from the Christmas tree glittering in the living room corner, she suddenly blurted out the news. "Oh, and by the way. A guy might stop by. Maybe on Christmas Eve."

Her mother smiled and didn't ask another question. But Sydney continued with a long explanation about a student who she was teaching to become a teacher, blah, blah, blah. The words didn't matter to her mother. She simply nodded and smiled again. The peanut brittle was bubbling like a thick wave of golden lava. Her mother carefully measured out the cups of raw peanuts to add to the mixture. Raw peanuts – that was the secret to really good peanut brittle her mother always said. They were bigger and didn't have an overdone burnt flavor like already roasted peanuts did.

"By the way. I forgot to tell you, he's Jewish," Sydney bit into a warm just out of the oven cookie and turned toward the living room to take a seat at the piano. That's done, she thought. Now we'll just see…

She fingered the sheet music spread across the piano and gazed at the tree with its decorations, lights and icicles. Dad always had to have the silvery icicles draped over each and every tiny needle. Above the front window was the traditional sixteen pointed white star made of paper that her Dad carefully assembled each year. It hung by a cord so the light bulb inside could shine through the pale thin paper points for the cars passing to notice. It was the traditional star of their protestant religion, and it made her heart relive all of the Christmases past. Christmas Eve was Dad's busiest day after weeks of endless preparation. The pageants, the choir concerts, the setting up of the crèche, and caroling – all traditions Sydney held dear not just personally, but as a family ... yes, family. She didn't want to think about Albert popping in and spoiling that tradition. He would never understand all of this. It would be completely foreign to his experiences.

Sydney slowly went back to the kitchen in time to watch her mother pour the golden liquid across the baking sheets. "Let me tell you what happened with Edward Garrett," Sydney began settling onto the stool once again.

Her mother nodded and listened as Sydney recounted the details of the photo shoot at Tara and the body found lying across the glass dance floor later. "It's eerie to think I might know or work with someone who might be a murderer," Sydney confessed. Then her mind went to Albert. She decided not to mention he was a suspect. But why was he a suspect? Had he really committed this murder and was now coming into her very home? She frowned. Had she put her family in danger? Of course not. She was his alibi. She had been with him the entire time after the shoot.

Finally, when her mother finished pouring the candy and gently carried the sheets to the stoop outside to cool, she asked, "Who do you think might have done this?" She wiped her hands on a dish towel tied to the cabinet handle.

"Well, Edward did make a lot of enemies it seems. He may have been a great dancer, but he wasn't a good businessman and his ego got in the way quite a bit. He owed everyone money, including most of the staff. I don't know that money would be a motive, however. With Edward dead, there would be no way to ever collect on a debt." Sydney rested her chin on her hand as she leaned in to smell the freshly baked cookie aroma.

"Did he owe you money? Are you having trouble financially?" Her mother's voice sounded more concerned than usual.

"Oh, Mom. Don't worry about me. I can live on nothing," Sydney laughed but thought inside to add "and I do live on nothing" but stopped. She, like most of the other staff members, lived quite simply. Sharing houses and apartments to save on rent, riding the bus to work rather than driving, and doing without some of the things other people took for granted. So who didn't live frugally? That might be something the police should look into. Who really lived above their means?

"What if it isn't someone who works at the studio?" Her mother brought up another possibility. The police were looking at all the people who were at the photo shoot. But what if it was someone who hadn't been there? The thought passed quickly and soon Sydney and her mother were laughing about other things. Edward Garrett and Albert Rothchild were forgotten.

Sydney pulled out the dress she packed from her small suitcase and hung it in the closet to smooth out any wrinkles before church. The evening would be packed with activity. Dad would have two services that evening, and the family had chosen to go to the second one. When they were young children, the family had always gone to the early service and then streaked home to get into pajamas and wait for Dad. They would sit patiently at the front window watching all of the cars from the second service drive away. Then peering into the darkness waited as Dad moved in slow motion from the front door of the church toward their own front steps. He always took as much time as possible to give that added drama before he opened the door. They would descend upon him with giggling delight, pleading with him to "hurry, hurry, hurry." But of course he always seemed to go even slower.

Tonight, they were all adults. It would be different. They would have no trouble waiting patiently for the exchange of gifts. The special moment instead would be their time together as a family sharing the traditions as they sat in the front row of the sanctuary and sang the traditional carols.

Dad would leave early to get ready for the first service, so dinner was almost ready - much earlier than the typical 6:00 time that stood as "dinner time" in the Monroe household. Sydney was already in her dress and helping Mom prepare the table for the rest of the family to eat, when the doorbell rang. "Sydney", the voice of her sister rang out.

Albert Rothchild drove slowly down the tree lined small town street. He clutched the tiny piece of paper Sydney Monroe had secretly placed in his hand after the last lesson they shared before the holiday. He squinted at the numbers hastily written and peered at each house until he finally located the large older home nestled behind a large pine tree. Parking across the street, he opened the door to his Cadillac and stood momentarily to gaze at the quiet street. What was he doing? He briefly closed his eyes, returned the paper to his pocket, and scurried across the street toward the well lit porch with the star in the window.

Sydney turned to see Albert Rothchild standing in the doorway. He was smiling nervously and carried a tin of store bought peanut brittle as a gift. Sydney almost laughed at the irony, but instead greeted him and invited him in for dinner. "Everyone, this is Albert," she introduced each member of her family and pulled out the chair on the corner of the table motioning for him to take a seat.

No one said anything. They didn't talk about the studio. Everyone simply sat at the table and enjoyed the chicken and mashed potatoes. Albert chatted as if he belonged to the family trying not to ask questions about "Christmas" that would embarrass him as a non-Christian. He dutifully came along to the second service and smiled as if he knew exactly what it all meant. Sydney admired his tactful approach to what must have been a very confusing evening.

When the service was over and they had returned home to begin the gift exchange, Albert presented his can of peanut brittle to Sydney's mother who graciously accepted it and passed it around for everyone to sample. They all smiled and nodded as they bit into the thin tasteless bits of candy with the overcooked roasted peanuts.

It grew later and later with no sign of Albert saying his farewell. So finally, Sydney's mother asked Albert if he would like to spend the night on the living room couch. He agreed with a smile and stretched out wrapped in a crocheted afghan that Sydney's mother had draped over the back. Sydney raised an eyebrow but said nothing but a quick goodnight. She pursed her lips and frowned as she closed the door to her room. He certainly was trying to fit in.

The next morning, he was chatting away at the kitchen table with her mother as he forked a corner of French toast off his plate. They both smiled at Sydney as she grabbed her favorite stool to join them. "Albert was just telling me about the studio," her mother said with a raised eyebrow and a smirk. "It seems to be quite an unusual place."

111

"Yes, it is," Sydney agreed shooting a look of curiosity towards Albert.

"Sheldon and Cary seem like good friends," her mother said setting a cup of coffee down in front of Albert. Neither Sydney's mother nor her father drank coffee, so Mom must have pulled out an old jar of instant to make for Albert. "Breakfast?" she asked Sydney as she turned to flip another piece of egg dipped bread into the pan.

Albert stayed all day and then spent the night once again on the living room couch. Sydney was beginning to wonder when he would leave. The time they spent with family was pleasant, but unusual. Everyone was on their best behavior asking Albert questions about himself and his own family. Sydney learned a whole lot about Albert that she hadn't known in all those years of teaching him dance lessons. The strange part for Sydney was Albert just included himself in their family and their holiday without so much as a thought that he might be imposing. And for some strange reason, it didn't feel like he was imposing.

By the third day, Albert asked Sydney if she needed a ride back to the cities. "No, I have my car," Sydney answered nodding out the window at the gold Demon parked on the street. "Oh, so that's your car," Albert said. "I guess I don't know everything about you after all."

"What's that suppose to mean? Oh, never mind. I'll see you in the studio later," Sydney retorted almost shutting the door in his face. She watched him walk slowly toward his car, glancing back to see if she was at the window.

"I hid the good peanut brittle," was all her Mom said as Sydney picked up her suit case and prepared to leave. "Have a good trip back. And be careful." Sydney nodded, then turned back to give her mother a long hug. It was if she were saying without words "if anything happens to me, you'll know why."

Sydney drove back to the cities with a few new thoughts. It would be another month until Albert was considered a full fledged teacher. She would have some serious decisions to make regarding their relationship. A month might seem like a long time now, but it wasn't really. What would she do about Todd? What would the rest of the staff think if anyone found out about the holiday visit? Things were getting way too complicated. It had all begun with Edward Garrett and his bright idea to bring in more business. His death had made it even more complicated. Sydney's stomach churned.

Mary Lou Smith was on the phone with Suzanna Caldwell. "How was the holiday season for the downtown studio?" She listened for a few moments and then briefly described the financial situation in the suburban studio. "We need to get together and discuss some of the studio finances. I learned from Larry Underhill that Edward still hasn't paid for the billboard. What do you propose we do about that? It's quite a large sum of money." Again she listened and then grabbing a pen nodded. "Right. That would work out. I'll put you on my calendar."

Sydney arrived back at the two story house she shared with Todd and his cousin. She parked the car in front of the house and for a few moments stared out at the lightly falling snow. The darkness shielded her from the world. She placed her forehead gently on the top of the steering wheel and hummed "Silent Night" in a low alto register. If only life would go along smoothly without all of the bumps. She could feel inside the rocky days that were ahead and there was a heavy feeling of dread. Was Albert a killer? No, that was impossible. Although no matter what she really thought, there would always be that small pang of doubt gnawing away at her stomach. And what about Todd? What would she do about Todd?

XV.

"Look who's here!" Morgan couldn't hide the surprise. Standing at the front desk was a muscular man in faded jeans, a bristling mustache and a tuft of facial hair just below his lower lip. Todd was always cheerful even though his forehead had a permanent furrow that gave the false impression he was troubled.

"Hey, what are you doing here?" Sydney looked around and motioned with her hand. "Here in the dance studio?"

"I decided to come in to take a few lessons." He grinned.

"Oh, are you 'Mr. Lear'?" Morgan squinted at her own hand writing.

"That's me," he chimed in with a lightness to tenor his voice.

"OK." Morgan dragged out the short word as she pulled out a clipboard with a questionnaire attached. She handed him a pen and ordered, "Then just fill this out for me, please." He snatched the board and retreated to the couch in the reception area to study the questions.

Sydney and Albert danced around the floor with Sydney taking a few quick glances at Todd and Megan laughing on their lesson. It was obvious to Sydney that

Albert had no idea who Todd was, and she meant to keep it that way. Todd stayed after the lesson for the group class. Megan had the beginning dancers doing some fun exercises to loosen up. Todd seemed to really get into all of the funny old dances Megan introduced. His Funky Chicken was especially entertaining. Sydney could hardly keep herself from laughing, but she managed to only allow a slight giggle.

"That was sweet," Morgan whispered to Sydney as she waved good-by to Todd. He would glance back over his shoulder with an impish grin as he slowly walked out the door and toward the elevators.

"Sweet," Sydney said but thought it was too late to take a sudden interest. She had almost made up her mind about Albert. At least she felt she should give him a chance when the time came. Yes, it was too late.

"Carson," she grabbed his arm. "Can I have a quick word with you?"

Carson Hunter lived a block away from Sydney and Todd in a large two story home he had purchased with a few of his college friends after they graduated. The four friends were anything but alike. Carson was totally immersed into his dancing and studio life. One of the women roommates was engaged to her college sweetheart, and the other a diehard lesbian. The fourth friend was clearly gay with a set of friends who enjoyed hanging out at the house after a night of bar hopping. Yes, it was an odd group in that house. Sydney had only become acquainted with them because her close proximity made Carson a frequent bus partner and car pool friend.

"Carson, I need a favor," Sydney began.

That evening with both arms struggling to drag her suitcases, Sydney arrived at Carson's doorstep with a splitting headache and a weary feeling all over. A few days apart from Todd might just give her a new perspective on her current problem. Carson hadn't asked the specifics, but had always felt close to Sydney. So he had of course said "yes" when she asked if she could spend a few days at his house.

The kitchen was overflowing with friends who were laughing and toasting each other for some sort of celebration. Sydney dragged her things up to the couch on the landing between the first and second floors. It didn't provide much privacy with people staggering up the stairway at all hours of the night, but it was a place to get away. The night was trying. Sydney woke with a case of laryngitis and a worse headache.

She slowly moved down the stairs in the morning and grabbed the wall phone in the kitchen. Dialing the number of the studio, she told Morgan she was sick and wouldn't be in.

After huddling under a quilt on the hall couch, the next day proved to be similar to the first. She again called in and crawled up to retake her place on the couch.

That evening as she tried to hide her head under the blanket from as the group of friends were once again partying in the kitchen, she was surprised to hear her name. It was Carson. He was standing at the top of the stairway with a troubled look on his face.

"What is it?" she grimaced angrily.

"You have a visitor," he announced blandly and clearly disturbed.

Climbing up the stairs behind Carson was Albert.

"I was worried about you," he began as he took a seat on the edge of the couch.

"Nothing to worry about. I'm just sick. Sick and I need some sleep. So if you wouldn't mind...". She hinted as respectfully as she could. She grabbed a tissue and dabbed her nose.

"I brought you something," he dismissed the hint and pulled out a tiny box.

"Oh, no," she thought as she gazed at the size of the small package.

He clicked open the box to display a beautiful gold ring with a diamond in the center of a serpentine heart.

She buried her head in the blanket and wailed, "I don't want it. I don't want it. Go away. Please, go away."

Albert looked shocked and rising from the couch made a hasty retreat down the stairs and out the door.

A moment later, Carson returned. This time instead of a soothing and calm demeanor, he showed an impatient side Sydney had never seen before. "My roommates are not happy with you being here. You need to leave, and you need to leave now."

Sydney stared at him in disbelief.

"I'm not happy with you being here either. I don't know what is going on in your life right now, but you can't hide out. You are sick because of all the things happening inside of you. Make some decisions right now and get on with life. That's my advice and I think you need to take it." He turned and abruptly stalked down the stairs back to the laughing guests seated in the kitchen.

Sydney quickly got up, refolded the blanket, and grabbed her bags for the clumsy decent down the stairs and out the door. In humble regret, she staggered back to

Todd's house. Todd was sitting on the couch as usual and greeted her as if nothing had happened. He had no questions about where she had been or why she was back. She realized that was the way their relationship had always been – supportive yet indifferent. She snuggled into his comforting arms and tried to put Albert out of her mind.

The next day she felt better. Things were settled. Her decision had been made. She was sorry Albert had agreed to pay so much money to Edward Garrett for the teacher training, but that was his problem and not hers. She had almost a smile on her face when she walked through the door ready to give Albert her decision. Then she waited at the front desk for their lesson. The studio was quiet.

"How are you doing?" Morgan asked as Sydney leaned on the desk top trying to see the clock Morgan had recently hidden below. Edward had never allowed clocks in the studio, but now that he was gone, Morgan had placed a small clock next to the booking sheets. Everyone noticed it but no one mentioned it.

"Better," Sydney said with a quick nod of the head. Was Carson right? Had this sickness come because of all the stress she was feeling? Could be. She twisted her mouth as she pondered his assessment of her condition. OK. So now it was ten minutes after 12 and still no Albert.

Of course, he was always late and scampering in at the last moment. Not unusual. Sydney tapped her foot impatiently then went out to the dance floor to warm up. She glanced at the lesson plan she had prepared in Albert's dance folder and tried a few quick pivots. Half an hour and still no Albert.

"Morgan, could you give Albert a quick call to make sure he didn't forget his lessons?" Sydney poked her head around the bricked barrier that hid the dance floor from the front desk.

"Forget? You must be kidding! He's had the same schedule for weeks! Sure... I'll call," she shook her head and began to look up the number in her file.

"Sorry. No answer," she reported after placing the phone back into its cradle. She shrugged her shoulders and gave a sorry look.

Albert didn't show up all day. Every time Sydney called his number it simply rang and rang – not even the answering machine picking up to take business calls. What could have happened here? She knew all too well what was happening. It was because of her rejection. It was because she had asked – no told him to leave last night. Where was he? What was he doing? This was not like Albert. Albert was a survivor. He had survived his fiancé and her unfaithfulness... Oh, no. Had she pushed Albert over the edge? Would he do something so dreadful as to kill himself over her rejection?

Several days passed and still no Albert. Sydney wasn't sick anymore; she was frantic. The minutes were almost unbearable. She questioned Cary and Kiki but neither of them had heard any word from Albert. Should they call the police?

Sydney leaned on the front desk. It was Thursday and still no word. "Morgan, I think we need to call the authorities." Sydney looked as if she hadn't slept in days – and she hadn't. Sickness followed by fatigue gave her a hollow gaunt appearance.

"OK. If that's what you want me to do," Morgan looked up grimly and then began to smile. She pointed to the door.

Sydney spun around to face Albert. He had just walked in. "Are you ready for our lesson?" he asked casually without so much as a twitch in his voice.

Sydney grabbed Albert and hugged him, then she dragged him back to Suzanna's small private office down the hallway. She quickly shut the door them and then let out a huge sigh and demanded, "You scared me to death. Where were you?" Then before he could answer she said,

"No. Don't tell me. I don't want to know. OK. Here is the deal. I was so worried about you that I began to realize how much you touch me. You bring out some kind of emotion in me that I can't explain. I want you to know I will be ending a very special relationship to have one with you. So it better not be a fly by night thing here. It had better be serious. And I mean serious, mister."

She had finished her speech all in one breath when without a second's hesitation, Albert went down on his knee and said, "Will you marry me?"

"Oh, my." She signed and stared at the floor for a moment pressing her fingertips to her closed eyelids before replying. "Yes, I will. Just pick a date, and I'll be there." Sydney felt elation as well as sadness. Edward Garrett had won. He was still controlling her life even in death. A shudder went through her body. Who would have anticipated this?

Now to deal with Todd. Todd, oh Todd, must be so confused. She was confused, and she was making the decisions and knew what had been happening. So he must really be confused. Tonight won't be a happy night. She turned to Albert. "I have no place to live. I have to move out of my home. And I have no money to rent a place on my own." Her arms hung at her side in total despair.

"I'll pick you up tonight at eleven. You can live in my house with me." Albert turned and walked out the door. A slight grin spread across his face and then quickly faded. "Time to dance," he announced calmly.

XVII.

The evening was unpleasant. Sydney spent the time in tears sitting on Todd's lap trying to explain everything without really explaining anything. "I'm sorry, I'm sorry," she had said through the salty drips. "I'm getting married, and it's not to you." He had nodded knowingly. It hadn't been as much of a shock as Sydney had anticipated. But the emotion was still very brittle. They both clung to each other and cried. He had suspected long ago she was emotionally gone. It was the dancing. He would always blame the dancing and the way it crept into a soul to control. He had never been a part of that studio and never would be.

At eleven o'clock on the dot, Albert had pulled up outside the house and waited as Sydney dragged all her bags once again out to the curb. He tossed them in the back of his work truck, and they sped off.

Albert's small house was a bit of a shock. It was completely empty. Sydney stared at the one story rambler in dismay. "I'll fix it up," Albert said as she dropped her bags in the entry way. "It'll look really nice, I promise," he sighed. She just shook her head and took a seat on the floor to review what she had just done. It had been a shocking day all around and her head sunk cradled in her open palms. As if not to notice the hunched posture of this distressed human, a Siamese colored long haired cat sauntered up, squeezed through the taunt arms, and curled up in Sydney's lap.

"Omar," Albert introduced.

"Omar," Sydney repeated and stroked the long but matted fur. The cat purred loudly. Life was going to be very different. Very different. Although totally exhausted, Sydney barely slept all night. Too many strange and different environments, Sydney concluded. No place was home.

Sydney's conversation with Suzanna the next morning was just as confusing as the end of the day before. Suzanna sat at her desk facing a stammering Sydney as she tried to explain just what was going on in her life. With her fingertips to her lips, Suzanna had taken in all of the information, viewed all of the spontaneous tears, handed over a few tissues, and sighed a good many times with eyes closed.

"Sydney, I can't condone what has happened here. Yet, I can't condemn you either. I myself am having a relationship with a student." She stopped abruptly and pointed a finger. "But if you say anything about this to anyone, I will deny it."

Sydney nodded and stared at the blank wall behind. Whoa!

Suzanna continued. "I am only confiding in you because I know the stress you are feeling at this very moment. My stomach is in knots, and I need to let it out to someone else. You, are that someone else."

Sydney didn't ask who the student was, nor did she offer any more information on her own situation. She remained silent – waiting.

"What else do you have to tell me? You look like you need to say more," Suzanna asked softly as she leaned across the desk and took one of Sydney's hands.

"We are getting married. It will be in another month. I'll give you the exact date in a day or two. The situation becomes more complicated because Albert is

Jewish. His family is very unhappy about me. They won't even meet me. It's been less than one day and already I'm an outcast. I had no idea the situation could be any more complicated than it appeared to be yesterday, but it is. I don't want to put Albert's relationship with his family in jeopardy. Yet, I have." Sydney shook her head with a regrettable sadness.

"What are you going to do about that?" Suzanna frowned as she took in the new details.

"Albert has a concert he is committed to play on Saturday night, but his family will all be gathering to celebrate an aunt and uncle's anniversary. I will be going to the party alone. I'll make my case to the family then."

"Were you invited? Do they know you are coming?" Suzanna's voice was now a horrified whisper.

"No. I do know one of Albert's uncles. He came to watch Albert perform at a few of the showcases we did last year. Hopefully, he will show some compassion and introduce me. If not, I don't know what I will do. I will be stuck at the world's worst party if they refuse to speak to me. I guess I'll have to deal with that if it happens." Sydney bowed her head and a small tear rolled down her cheek. Suzanna reached for another tissue to add to the mounting pile already accumulating on the desktop.

"Let's not say anything about this situation to the rest of the staff until you announce the wedding date. That will be coming up soon anyway. We can wait a few days – maybe until after the family gathering to see what happens. Let's get Albert through his dance tests and on the staff as quickly as we can." Suzanna nodded and peered up at the ceiling to think. "Oh, yes, and please no mention of my situation to anyone either." Sydney's head nodded up and down as she wiped the tears away with the fresh tissue. "Ok, let's get on with our day," Suzanna said firmly and rose from her seat. Her soft patterned skirt topped with a ruffled blouse and her usual strappy Latin heels in a calf skin black moved with a hushed swish down the hall to the reception area – a silent reminder of the pain the two were experiencing at this very moment.

At the front desk, heavy cardboard boxes were stacked along the reception room wall. Suzanna threw up her hands as if to ask, "What's all this?" Morgan grinned and held up an album cover. The albums were completed and there in all his splendor was Edward Garrett circling his arm around Amanda. Her head was tossed back with an enchanting smile as her disco tail splayed back behind her curls. The skirt she wore draped softly and the small bag wrapped around her waist sparkled. Edward had his usual cheeky grin. His cream suit looked sharply in contrast to the dark movement of the dancers in the background. Suzanna sucked in a loud gulp of air as she thought of Edward and that fateful day of shooting. This cover would always be a dreadful reminder.

"Here's another one," Morgan held up the cover with Antoine and Charlotte. "And another." Becca and Daniel looked fabulous.

The album covers were the subject of the day - everyone peering at the dark backgrounds to find themselves, the students "oohing" and "aahing" at the shots, and sad feelings that crept in as they gazed at the final photos of Edward Garrett. Sheila was the only one to snatch up a cover and sneer at the photo without her in the forefront. She wasn't even one of the shadowy dancers in the background who was recognizable. Was she positioned so far back in the crowd that her mass of hair wasn't even visible? It would appear so. She flipped the cover over the front desk and stalked off.

Needless to say, Sydney and Suzanna soon forgot the problems that weighed so heavily this morning. The albums lifted spirits yet also acted as a reminder that somewhere out there was a killer who had taken away a life. This case was unsolved and despite everyone having their own issues to deal with, they needed to join together and solve a murder.

Suzanna was on the phone with Mary Lou to let her know about the albums. "So, just what are we to do with so many albums?" Mary Lou demanded when given the news.

"I think these are our copies to do as we please. I'm sure Edward made some kind of a deal to give us a certain number over and above the ones the record company will be selling. That only seems logical." Suzanna summarized her limited knowledge of the situation.

"And the payment? Will the studio be getting paid so we can discuss getting a check to Larry for the billboard? I want to get this settled." Mary Lou's tone was firm.

"Has Larry been keeping up with his lessons?" Suzanna asked cautiously.

"Not since the breakfast we had to discuss finances," Mary Lou said with a weariness to her voice.

"Sorry," Suzanna sympathized.

"I should have known better." That was Mary Lou's last remark about the subject. It was on to further discussions about the studio and all the new infos coming in from the advertising.

XVIII.

Albert had kept his promise. In the course of a few days, he had managed to repaint the living room, bedrooms, and kitchen area. In fact, he had wallpapered the kitchen in a sort of jungle motif with green vined walls and orange cupboards. In spite of the strange color combinations, Sydney had to agree it was strangely elegant and put together. The living room was a three toned - white and Kelly green with a black accent stripe. There was a new black modern futon with a glass étagère complete with black, green and white vases and bookends complementing each shelf. Albert had put up new blinds and thrown a contemporary patterned throw rug across the wood floor. He had pulled up the old orange shag carpet that had been in every room and finished the floors.

"Wow!" was all that Sydney could say. "How could you do this in such a short time? You did do this yourself, didn't you?"

"Yup, all by myself," Albert nodded with pride in his voice. "When I take on a project, I really take on a project."

"I'll say you do!" Sydney gazed at the bedrooms each done in a flattering shade of lavender or green. The green room had floor to ceiling strips of mirror along one corner making the room appear much larger than before. "I'm very impressed."

"Thank you," Albert said with an almost embarrassed shake of his head. "I have a few more talents than you realized. Not just a great dancer..." he grinned waiting for the compliment to be returned.

"Not just a great dancer," Sydney smiled and continued her tour of the newly renovated rooms. Occasionally, Albert begged out of a day of lessons claiming he had work to do. Although, Sydney knew he had work to complete for his fish business, she recognized that this week's work was not related to business but to home improvements. It had been a few days worth the effort.

"We got the albums in the studio. Boxes of them," she mentioned as she peered around the kitchen.

"Did they turn out? How about any clues? Did they reveal anything about Edward's death?" Albert seemed anxious. He knew it was important to solve this murder – personally, it was important.

"Clues? I hadn't thought about that. Maybe tomorrow we'll have to look through all of the photos more closely. We could ask to see all of the pictures and not just the ones that made the covers." She suggested.

"Good idea!" Albert made a mental note to find out about the whole shoot. "Are you still planning to go to the anniversary party on Saturday?"

"Absolutely. And by the way, we need to get you through your bronze dance test ASAP. Suzanna said we have to get you on the staff right away. So don't spend all of your time with the house. Practice your patterns, please," Sydney begged.

"I will," Albert promised.

XIX.

It was Saturday morning – lazy and starting to feel like spring. Antoine Hawks ambled along the uptown area street with a baseball cap over his curls and a large pair of sunglasses covering his face. With a high turtle neck sweater pulled up over his chin and baggy jeans, it was difficult to image this was the same man dressed in the usual three piece suit every day in the studio. The look was soft and casual. He was out of his neighborhood and glancing at some of the unusual shop windows before spotting a quaint coffee shop on the corner of a well traveled street. Digging his hands into his pants pockets, he saw a crowd beginning to form outside and got in line for a cup of coffee and breakfast pastry.

The shop was small inside but opened to an outdoor area with clusters of wooden tables and shrubs creating a private patio for customers to enjoy their food, drink, and conversation. As he waited in line, Antoine glanced out the swinging door trying to spot a secluded table that might be free once he got his coffee. His scanning eyes spotted Larry Underhill seated at a table along a hedge. Larry was also dressed more casually than usual so Antoine actually passed over Larry a few times before registering exactly who he was. The gleaming smile was the tip off. Larry was dressed in a charcoal grey sweater with matching creased dress pants. Today there was no flower in the lapel, but the crisp white dress shirt peeking out from the top of the sweater completed a dressy casual look that was more recognizable than Antoine's baggy attire. Antoine squinted to see who the woman was seated across from Larry. She had a sleek dark up do and a slim classic dress covered by a suit jacket.

"I guess that would be Larry Underhill's type," Antoine murmured. Then grabbing his coffee and raspberry scone debated whether he should chance running into Larry by going out into the patio area. He glanced around to see a tall stool opening up along the inside wall and sauntered over to claim it before anyone else could. He sat down with his back to the door and snatched up a discarded newspaper from the corner. It felt good to have such a relaxing morning. The last few days...weeks had been so hectic. With Edward's death and all of the calls from the publicity of not only that story that but the new billboard, Antoine's days had been chaos. He was constantly on Suzanna's case trying to speed up the training process. He desperately needed some new teachers to keep up with the huge volume of new students. And Sheila was worthless. She still hadn't figured out the training program and its inclusion of her advanced students. Oh, well. She'd get it sooner or later. Although he had his claim in for a few of the new trainees, he knew Mary Lou would be just as desperate and would fight him tooth and nail for any of the new recruits. It was to his benefit that he knew them all first hand before the choices could be made. He could find the ones who would best fit with his current staff and really come out with some good new student department teachers.

The line for orders had slowed down as it got closer to noon, and Antoine glanced back to see if the patio – and Larry Underhill – had cleared. He was looking forward to a lazy relaxing day with absolutely nothing pressing to do.

That's when he saw Larry stand with mouth gaping as he began a heated conversation with his lady friend. He didn't bother to shove in his chair, just abruptly stormed out of the patio and into the street.

Antoine was a bit surprised to see that kind of emotion in the usually calm and controlled Larry Underhill, so debated for a moment if he should stroll into the patio and find out who this mystery woman might be. Not that he would know who she was. Larry certainly traveled in a very different circle of friends than those at the studio. Just as Antoine decided he was going to move from the inside to the outside area, he saw the woman stand and turn. She smiled slyly and put her sunglasses on as she sauntered up to the door. It was Greta Rothe. How different she looked today. Put together and sophisticated with such a businesslike appearance. What could Greta Rothe be doing with Larry Underhill? What did Greta Rothe do anyway? Was her business at all related to the ABC Advertising? Antoine made a note to himself to check through her studio records to find some answers to this one. It certainly was puzzling. Greta passed by Antoine without so much as a glance. She certainly wasn't expecting to see him just as he found it surprising to see her.

The time crept by slowly for Sydney Monroe as she debated what to wear to the anniversary party. What would be most appropriate? It was a mystery to her. Finally she selected a dress that was modest yet classic in design. Was this whole thing a mistake? It seemed her whole last year had been a huge mistake. She had ended one relationship abruptly and started a new one that was plunging into marriage. Then again there was Edward's death. What else could happen? She slowly put on her makeup and combed through her hair.

"Are you ready for this?" Albert asked as she slid into the passenger side of the car. "You don't have to do this, you know."

"Yes, I do." That was all she said and sat silently for the short drive to the two story brick house in an older section of town. The street was already lined with parked cars as Albert pulled up. He pulled up along side a parked car and waited.

"Do you want me to come in with you?" he nodded his head toward the front door.

"No. I think it's best if I do this alone." And she was out of the car and on her way up the front walk. It seemed like an eternity to get to that front door. Her black dress suddenly felt tight and clingy. She stopped for a moment and said a quick prayer before ringing the doorbell. A young girl opened the door and stared at her.

"Hi. I'm Sydney Monroe," Sydney put out her hand and the surprised girl slowly but reluctantly shook her hand. Well, that worked out OK, thought Sydney as she slid past into the large living room already filled with people. Faces began to turn and stare at her as she walked bravely through to the dining room where she spotted a seated old woman in the center of the floor. This must be one of Albert's grandmothers. He had told her all of the names, but just at this moment, they all seemed to disappear from her memory. She walked up to the seated woman and leaning over a bit to her level, Sydney introduced herself. The woman smiled, and Sydney smiled back. The woman's face crinkled as she gazed up at the young woman and in spite of her tiny almost bony appearance, she sat regally like a queen on her throne. It was evident that the "subjects" in the room treated her like royalty – everyone staring to see the reaction to this uninvited intruder. At this moment, there seemed to be acceptance. She probably didn't know who she was.

Someone tapped Sydney on the shoulder, and she glanced over to see Uncle Ben standing behind her. She had met Ben several times at some of the studio functions.

"You are a brave girl," he whispered. The Grandmother also smiled at his remark. Oh yes, this woman knew who Sydney was. Rumors obviously spread like fire through this family. "I'll introduce you if you would like." The Grandmother seemed to be fine with his suggestion. Ben looked around at all of the staring faces and made a quick head motion to his left side.

"It was nice to meet you," Sydney said to the grandmother. "I'll be back after I've met some more of the family." The grandmother smiled back and nodded. She looked frail and tiny, but Sydney knew from what Albert had told her this woman was as hard as nails. Married three times with three sets of children by those husbands who had each died before her, she had survived traveling from Russia to the United States just before World War II. She was the center of the family and her word was law. Her mind was sharp – clear as a crystal pool.

Standing in the corner of the room was a robust couple. The rotund gentleman had a mass of curly hair that haloed his cherub face, and the woman although not quite so round had vibrant red curls and a pinched expression. Albert's parent - Uncle Ben whispered.

Uncle Ben slowly led her across the room to the couple and without saying a word motioned for her to introduce herself to them. A second of time flew by before Albert's father reached out to embrace her. They stood in that embrace for what seemed an eternity with Albert's mother joining in the hug. Tears were streaming down his mother's face so there was even more to the pinched expression.

After a few words of greeting, the two led Sydney around to introduce the rest of the extended family and to the food table. Albert's mother began to babble on about each of the traditional Jewish dishes and how they were made. She loved to talk and seemed quite relieved to be able to finally explain tradition to a non-Jew. Her constant chatter wasn't really annoying, but rather soothing. It made Sydney feel safe and over the dreaded frightening initial fear she had experienced when walking through that front door.

A man with dark salt and pepper hair and a slight mustache came up to introduce himself. "I'm Sam. You are from the dance studio, am I right? I'm Cary Prang's uncle. I'm married to Albert's Aunt Marge." He nodded across the room to a pleasant dark haired woman chatting with an elderly woman. "We both have grown children from other spouses who have passed away. Mine ten years ago, and Marge's about seven years now."

Sydney began to study the man. "Are you surprised to find that I am a relative to Cary? We are a close community and many of the studio dancers are part of that community as well." He paused as if trying to remember names then continued, "Sheldon Stein lives just down the street. His parents have been friends of ours since we were youngsters. And Greta Rothe also went to school with the boys, I believe. Ben said he saw her at one of the dance parties. She's a strange one, that girl is." He shook his head leaving Sydney waiting for an explanation.

Finally he said, "When Albert's engagement broke off, such a sad day," he wagged his head back and forth and sucked in a breath of air. "When that engagement broke off, Greta was all over Albert. Of course, she had been chasing Cary for a good many years too. I'd be careful of that one now that you are engaged to Albert. You never know what she will do. The stories I've heard... of course, they could be just that, stories. People sometimes exaggerate when they tell a story." He smiled and directed Sydney over to introduce her to Marge.

After meeting most of the guests, Sydney ambled back to Albert's grandmother and pulling up a chair began to chat. Evidently the woman was left alone for most of the party whether from fear or from neglect, Sydney suspected

141

it was a little of both. The woman seemed pleased with the attention. She told Sydney about all of her own children and some of their accomplishments. Albert's father was her youngest and certainly seemed to be a favorite. "Baubie", as she was called, spoke of her youngest son's wonderful talents as a singer and actor. "Of course, all of his children share his love of the arts. Albert with his music, and Joseph with his acting." She smiled and seemed to recall in her mind some of their accomplishments. "Are you talented like that as well?"

"Well, I am a dancer. So I suppose that is an art – not quite like playing an instrument, but I move to music and entertain people. So it is quite similar," Sydney nodded.

"And is my grandson Albert a good dancer?"

Sydney smiled. "Yes, he is quite good. Not as good as I am of course…" and they both laughed sharing a quick sparkle of women's humor.

Placing a hand with a slight tremor on top of Sydney's hand, she leaned in so their faces were close. "I like you a lot. I'm glad you will be a part of this family. We need someone like you to give us heart."

When Albert came to pick up Sydney, his father and mother walked out to the car before Sydney. Sydney was saying her good-bys to his grandmother and other relatives. She tried to glance around to see what was happening with Albert and his parents, but they were huddled into a close triangle.

"You seem to have been the hit of the party," he proudly commented when she got into the passenger side of the car. She only nodded and leaned back into the seat to relax. As she glanced over his silhouette was pensive and a tear rolled down his cheek. He quickly brushed it away – the darkness in the car almost hiding the motion completely.

XX.

Suzanna spread the glossy prints across her desk and hunched over each with the eye of a reporter. Her sleek bob swung forward hiding her delicate face. She motioned Sydney to join her. It was early in the day and only the two of them were in the studio.

"I thought I'd ask for all of the shots taken from the Tara shoot. Maybe something important will jump out," she shrugged in way of explanation. "This whole situation is beginning to feel creepy. It's been too long since the police have had any leads or any viable suspects. That's

143

not good for this studio or the people who work here." Suzanna shook her head and crossed her legs leaning back away from the stack of photos. She glanced over at Sydney. "So what's the news? How was the weekend with the parents?"

"Actually, it turned out to be a very nice situation. I was so nervous." She sighed loudly and slunk down in a straight back chair with a little more stretching out of her legs into a more comfortable position. "But it all worked out very well. I met everyone. They seemed to accept me much better than expected and things are heading full steam ahead."

"You still look worried," Suzanna commented with a frown with a quick glance away from the photos.

"Well, how would you feel if your fiancé was the only suspect the police have focused on in a murder investigation? Comfortable about the wedding?" Sydney twisted her mouth and leaned forward. "Solving this murder would certainly help, now wouldn't it?"

Suzanna nodded her head in agreement and with a slender delicately boned hand reached out to study a photo. She shook her head. "The background shots are really dark," she passed the photo on to Sydney and reached for another one.

"You know we really should consider the possibility that maybe the murderer wasn't at the shoot. Maybe the place and time was chosen because everyone at Tara would be considered suspects." Sydney glanced at Suzanna for her reaction. Her large round glasses bounced as she whipped her head around and pursed her lips. She seemed to be taking in this consideration with great care.

"So who wasn't there? Who wasn't there!" Suzanna snatched up a few more photos and stared. "OK. Let's rule out people. Who had alibis and who wasn't there to provide an alibi?" She quickly ticked off each staff member, who they had carpooled with and when they had arrived at the studio. Everyone from the studio seemed to have an alibi. They had all traveled together except Amanda Garrett, Edward's ex-wife. She, of course hadn't come back to the studio after the shoot. So who knows what her alibi could have been, but certainly the police would have checked that out immediately. An ex-wife! First and foremost on the suspect list certainly.

"Listen, can we continue with this conversation this afternoon? I have a lesson with Derek Halvorson at noon," Sydney stood and began to smooth her skirt in front. She felt a little haphazard this morning. It still felt as if she were on a long trip and living out of a suit case. Nothing was in its correct place at Albert's house so her outfit was – well awkward. A wrinkled skirt she had put together with a blouse that didn't really match. It was all she could do this morning until she could get her things more organized. She shook her head as she glanced at her image in the mirror.

"And how is Derek doing?" Suzanna questioned with a smile. Derek was the son of a Minnesota dance legend. Etta Halvorson was every dancer's mentor. She had single handedly brought the dance world to the forefront in the arts community in Minnesota. Her dance troop and choreography were legendary. Derek, the son, was tall, good looking and at the age of twenty five, still single. "Has his mother's abilities rubbed off on him?"

Sydney laughed. "Unfortunately, no. He is such a nice, polite man. But his dance talents …well, let's just say he needs major help." Sydney shrugged and added a quick, "But he's fun to teach and extremely eager to learn."

The dance floor was empty. It was too early for the rest of the staff to have lessons scheduled. Morgan Canfield had just settled herself behind the desk tapping her foot to the beat of a newly popular disco song blaring from the stereo system. She glanced to her right at the image of the two dancers in the mirror. Sydney and Derek were dancing a fast disco swing hustle exchanging places as they danced in a slot movement. Hands joined, the arms raised and lowered allowing fast turns as each dancer glided into the spot of his/her partner. Morgan smiled and resumed her attention to the schedule for the day when she heard a light thud. Glancing up again she saw the image in the mirror had changed. Sydney Monroe was down on the floor, and Derek was frantically bending over her.

Morgan rushed to the dance floor. "What happened? Did she faint?" she saw Sydney's head drop back and blood spurting from her lip as it quickly began to swell.

"We were just dancing…oh, my. What did I do? I didn't mean to hit you. I jabbed her with my elbow as she was coming under the arms to do her turn." Derek was frantic, apologizing and trying to mop up the blood with his shirt sleeve.

"Here," Morgan said quickly. "Let me get some paper towels from the bathroom." She hastened to snatch a stack of towels and began to hold them to Sydney's puffy lip as Derek dabbed at the floor now red with blood. "I think she's OK." Morgan tried to reassure Derek who by this time was beside himself with remorse. "Everything is going to be just fine," Morgan said over and over again.

"Derek! Derek! I'm good." Sydney was just beginning to realize what had happened. Her eyes lids fluttered. Everything had moved so quickly that she was just reliving the fateful blow in slow motion. Yes, the elbow had bam! Just hit her square in the face – the mouth to be exact. She had fallen back and somehow was now lying on the floor in a pool of blood. "It really looks much worse than it actually is," Sydney tried to reassure Derek. "You just go have some lunch and don't worry about a thing. "

Morgan had scurried to the kitchen to get a towel full of ice and was now gently pressing the cold cloth to Sydney's lip. She held a fistful of paper towels to remop the blood spattered floor. Derek's blotting had only made the floor appear worse than it was with blood streaked along the floor boards and drying in thin coated patches.

"My heavens, what happened here?" Suzanna had sauntered out to the front desk and spied the trio clustered together in the center of the dance floor.

"Oh, we are just fine now, aren't we Derek? Just a slight problem with a turn that's all," Sydney had now gotten up off the floor and was guiding Derek toward the front door. "I'll see you next week. Same time, OK?" He nodded, eyes still glazed over.

148

"He won't be back, will he," Morgan whispered.

"Nope," Sydney replied. And he never did return just as predicted.

Sydney grabbed Suzanna's hand and dragged her back to the tiny office.

"What about Larry Underhill? He certainly didn't return to the studio. He must have been alone. When did he return to his office? Does he even have an office?" Sydney spouted out the questions as they came to mind. "You know I have been thinking about the reason for the police to suspect Albert. We know there was something at Tara that pointed to him. Something on that dance floor. Maybe something dropped. Or a last minute clue provided by Edward before he died. Like maybe he wrote something on the glass floor... in blood." She pressed the ice pack to her lip.

"You look awful," Suzanna grimaced. "You mean he wrote words with his blood on the dance floor?"

Sydney nodded. "But in spite of whatever was there, the police dismissed Albert after he provided an alibi. Why? Maybe the clue could point to someone else. Edward wouldn't have enough energy or time to write 'Albert' or 'Rothchild'. Way too long. But maybe he wrote something else. Like initials. AR. AR like in the word LARry? Maybe some of the letters were missing and the only thing they could clearly read were the AR. Or maybe the 'L' looked like a line or a 1. What do you think of that theory?"

"Larry Underhill. He wasn't at the shoot, and your theory could be possible." Suzanna chewed her bottom lip. "But what motive would there be? Why would Larry kill Edward Garrett?"

"We have no idea what the agreement was between Larry and Edward, do we? There could have been more to the whole thing that we don't know anything about." Sydney was suddenly standing up tall. Her chin stretched forward. She tapped lightly on a glossy photo still stacked on Suzanna's desktop. "Whatever the reason, we need to find a way to clear Albert before this wedding."

"Well, I have a proposal," Suzanna whispered.

The wedding was scheduled in four weeks. They would hold the event in a hotel managed by Albert's mother. The family, although newly excited by the plans, could not accept a religious ceremony – either Jewish or Christian. Sydney and Albert understood and had agreed to the Rothchilds' request.

Sydney and Suzanna strolled through a number of stores along the mall. "I have only one task," Sydney laughed. "And that is to pick out a dress for the wedding. Albert is taking care of all the other details. I'm afraid I'm not even very good at my one and only responsibility," she sighed as she fingered a few dresses hanging on a rack in a discount store.

"Does that have underlying psychological implications? Are you looking forward to this at all? Don't you even want a traditional wedding gown?" Suzanna had agreed to come along to help choose something appropriate. When Sydney had strolled into a store not normally associated with weddings, Suzanna began to feel a little confused. She shook her head but followed along fingering a few dresses as she passed the racks.

"I'm too practical. This dress should be something I can wear over and over again. It can't be a big white bubble that I pack up and store for the next fifty years. It has to be something I can dance in or wear for another occasion. Let's check out the sale rack." She added with a sly grin, "I'm also very poor."

They both laughed. Sydney held up a few selections and headed to the dressing room to try on her choices. She finally decided on a lacy full length dress with an off the shoulder ruffle in cream. And the price was only thirty dollars – a steal of a price. "Now that wasn't too bad, was it?" she remarked holding up the dress for approval. "It even looks weddingy."

The studio would host a pre-wedding party for staff and students. Sydney and Albert certainly couldn't invite everyone to the wedding ceremony as it would be a smaller family affair. But they knew people would feel slighted if they weren't included, so Suzanna and Antoine Hawks had suggested the studio throw a party for everyone. It would include music and dancing. It would be a time to celebrate since so little of that had been a part of studio life since the death of Edward Garrett. Hopefully, it would be a time of renewal and moving on. Both studios could share in the festivities. Suzanna thought it would be the perfect occasion to gather all of the most logical suspects in Edward Garrett's murder as well - although she didn't share this part of the plan with anyone other than Sydney.

Sydney had been in the studio since early morning helping with decorations and teaching a few students during the afternoon and early evening hours. Her lip had caused a stir. Some students at first had whispered about a domestic assault, but the staff had been quick to let everyone know it was a work related accident with a student turning his teacher improperly. The whole incident had even become the subject of several group lessons – how to turn a lady with control.

But now, Sydney retreated to the back teachers' office to change into a floating tea length dress in off-white with a pale blue sash. She had once used the dress for a Waltz routine and relished the opportunity to wear it again. She lifted the skirt to sit for a moment in Suzanna's empty office. Her strappy dance shoes were lying on the floor as she checked her watch. She had a few minutes until they had to be cinched onto her tired feet. Suzanna peeked in and carefully checking the hall behind her, slid in and closed the door.

"How are you feeling?" Suzanna stood let her hand cover her mouth as she always did when nervous. Sydney nodded. "Everything is set. Mary Lou has invited Larry Underhill to be her escort to the party tonight. It's now or never. We have to confront him about the murder. Do you think you can do this?"

"I have to." Sydney put her head down in thought. "This has to be solved now. Do we have the plan down? I haven't told Albert anything about this. Just you and me. You didn't tell Mary Lou why you wanted her to invite Larry did you?"

Suzanna shook her head no. "But I did ask her to be especially attentive to Larry as we wanted him to feel comfortable. I told her to stick to him like glue - that we needed him for future advertising plans. She didn't ask any questions, but I suspect she knows we are planning something. She's too smart not to think something is strange about the whole request."

With her shoes buckled and a final glance into the wall mirror to make sure the make-up was covering the still evident bruise on her upper lip, Sydney waited for Albert to arrive so they could greet people together in the studio's reception area. Albert looked so handsome and yet so normal in his tux – a tux was his usual attire when he played his music. So his was made perfectly for him and not like the typical man who looked and felt uncomfortable in an ill-fitting rented suit that hung here and pulled up there. They looked the charming couple.

Morgan Canfield sat at the desk and called out greetings to students who began to arrive. She gave a special nod and smile to Sydney and Albert as they came down the hallway. There was even a touch of blush on her normally doughy cheeks and a spot of lip gloss on her clamped mouth. There was Rumba music playing in the background and a few teachers on the floor dancing. Mary

Lou Smith entered clinging to the arm of a very dapper Larry Underhill. Larry wore an exquisite red rose in his lapel and flashed a charming grin at Morgan. Morgan returned the smile and noticed how tiny Mary Lou looked alongside Larry. She gripped his arm tightly as if she needed his support before guiding him into the ballroom.

Excusing herself from Albert's side, Sydney strolled out to the dance floor and positioned herself next to Mary Lou and Larry. "I hope you don't mind, but could I borrow Mary Lou for a quick moment?" Sydney leaned forward catching Larry's eye and gripping Mary Lou's arm pulling her toward Suzanna's tiny back office. Larry, of course, flashed his handsome smile and nodded graciously excusing them.

"What is this all about?" Mary Lou hissed as they scooted down the hallway with Mary Lou in front. She turned and pursing her lips together demanded, "I need to ask you something. Do you love him?"

Sydney dropped her eyes and answered, "I can't answer you. I don't know."

"You are going to marry this man, and you don't even know if you love him?" Mary Lou placed her fists on her hips and led the way into Suzanna's office glancing into the wall mirror to catch Sydney's reaction.

Sydney leaned against the doorway and sighed. "It's just that I am not quite sure…".

She was interrupted by a hooded face peering around the door frame. The black floor length cape and heavy hood made Mary Lou gasp in surprise. Sydney turned to see the dark silhouette of Greta Rothe standing behind her. How she had managed to glide down the hallway without so much as the scuff of a shoe and catch the two of them off guard was anyone's guess. The hood draped over her dark greasy bangs and the dark shadowy lids of her eyes were coated in thick black liner.

"You!" she hissed pointing a finger from the front drape of the cape.

"I'm sorry," pleaded Sydney. "Did I do something to offend you?"

"Not you," Greta glared and then turned her face toward Mary Lou who was still standing with her back to the door. Mary Lou was short and tiny with a matronly figure. Her hair was cut in a crisp short sophisticated style and her navy dress was well tailored. But despite her put together appearance, Mary Lou's face went ashen and she began to hunch forward as if to shrink away from that finger still stretched in her direction. "You know what you did!" The hiss was loud and sinister. Then the caped woman was gone as if in a puff of smoke.

"What did you do?" Sydney dabbed her pulsing lip as she looked around to view an instantly empty hallway.

"Honestly, I have no idea. I don't have a clue," Mary Lou was now turned and her cheeks looked hollow. She closed her eyes and inhaled deeply.

"What's wrong?" Albert came scurrying down the hall. "What happened?" Albert was not a man who took long striding steps; he scurried on his two little legs reaching the two women quickly.

"Did you see Greta?" Sydney asked nervously.

"No. What did Greta do? Did she threaten you?" He pulled up to his full height with his chin jutting out and his eyes slit into a menacing frown.

"No, she threatened Mary Lou," Sydney pointed to Mary Lou and cocked her head to the side as if pondering the situation. "She threatened Mary Lou," she repeated.

"Very odd," Albert pondered. Then they both stared at Mary Lou who at this point didn't really notice the fact that people were even looking at her.

Albert escorted the two shaking women back to the dimly lit reception area. The ballroom was dark and music was playing. Dancing people were crowding the floor.

Sydney guided Mary Lou back to Larry Underhill. Her mission for this evening had been forgotten. It was hard to brood when festive music is playing and the people are laughing. Greta's threat was soon an event in the past. Albert assured Mary Lou that "Greta is just strange that way. Nothing Greta does ever has a good explanation." All was forgotten.

Cary Prang and KiKi Mays began to laugh hysterically when Sydney tried to explain to them what had happened. "That's nothing," Cary said and told a couple of stories about Greta stalking other students. "Now that was scary," he proclaimed when he told about the time she followed someone home on the city bus and stood outside their home next to a tree for a few hours just staring at the house.

"And how do you know this?" Sydney demanded.

"Because I was the one she was following," KiKi whispered. "It was very scary."

"Did you ever find out the reason for her unusual behavior?" Sydney's eyes opened wider.

"Never. And I don't think I ever will," KiKi shook her head and shrugged. "I just try to stay away from her if possible."

Suzanna eased around the corner of the reception desk to take her place at the two chest high bongo drums Edward always used each dance party to beat along with the music. They reached a bit higher on her tiny frame allowing her to rest her elbow and finger her chin and lips like Jack Benny used to do when thinking. She gazed across the floor to where Sydney, Albert, Cary and KiKi were huddled in the corner. Their animated conversation vacillated between head back laughter to troubled frowns. Suzanna had briefly heard the tale of Greta and her accusations so she assumed their conversation was surrounding that event.

Her eyes moved on to Mary Lou looking smaller and more fearful than usual. Mary Lou was usually as hard as nails – both in her look and her body language. She usually stood tall and in control with an arrogant spirit to her gaze that boor through another person like an arrow. Tonight she clung to Larry Underhill's arm eyes to the floor. Larry remained strong and confident with his white teeth glistening even in the dark room.

Antoine Hawks was twirling around the room with an older student. His giddy laughter cut the heaviness in the air. Sheila stood in the corner with her arms crossed and a chilly glare at someone across the floor. The story of

Greta and her shrouded threats had passed from student to student and teacher to teacher. Suzanna watched the rumor spread like a wave through the room. Some gasped, others laughed as if it were no surprise, and some just shook their heads in disbelief. Suzanna remained frozen in her pose, fingers gently stroking her lips. Her eyes watched as her mind was quickly processing the scene and the people. The plan hadn't worked. Her right hand began to draw on the cover of the bongo – "AR, AR". Maybe not "AR". She liked Larry Underhill. He hadn't deviated from the person she had first met. Was it a cover or was Larry Underhill just a great people loving person who genuinely liked everyone he met? Hmmm. She decided he really did like everyone he met.

"Mary Lou," Suzanna pulled her aside before she could walk out the door. "I'm sorry you had a confrontation with Greta. What was that all about?'

"I wish I could tell you. I have no idea what she was thinking. It's very confusing as well as scary." Mary Lou shook her head. "I haven't even spoken to that woman except to smile and say hello in my usual charming way."

Suzanna laughed. "You certainly are charming," Suzanna agreed with a sly knowing smile. Mary Lou could be cold and crisp in her approach to people, but now was not the time to mention that little criticism. "So you've had no other contact with Greta than through, say a studio party situation?"

"None whatsoever! That's why this is so startling to take in. I think she's just a nut case. That's what I think," Mary Lou concluded.

"You know, I think when you go to Sydney and Albert's wedding – you are going, aren't you?" Suzanna fished.

"Well, yes. I suppose I will have to," Mary Lou grumbled.

"Ask Larry Underhill to be your date. You need to have someone to protect you." Suzanna made the suggestion with a nod of the head.

"Is that witch going to be at the wedding? I thought we agreed students wouldn't be invited," Mary Lou's voice was hard.

"Well, there are a few students who are close friends of Albert's. He was after all a student himself. That would be a natural assumption. We can't dictate who someone should invite to their own wedding, now can we?" Suzanna put her hands on her hips in anticipation of an argument. She had known Mary Lou way too long. But Mary Lou had had a long night already and simply let it go without so much as a whimper. She began to search out Larry who was in the corner chatting with Antoine and a new student Antoine was trying to introduce to as many people as possible. Larry was his normal charming self, and the new student was intrigued with his magnetic smile and positive encouragement for her dance future. "You'll love it, I guarantee that," Larry promised as Mary Lou snatched at his sleeve to let him know she was ready to leave. "By chance did you see our billboard?" Mary Lou began to tug more forcefully. The student remained in a dreamy trance as the two walked out the front door ahead of her.

Suzanna smiled. Now for a little research before the wedding day.

XXI.

"Are you happy with the dress?" Sydney hung the garment on the hook in the corner and removed the bag the store clerk had draped over for protection. The dress had the same off the shoulder ruffle that Sydney had chosen for her bargain wedding gown. This dress was quite a bit pricier but had a similar style without all of the lace. The

162

silken fabric was a lush berry color and would compliment Suzanna's skin tone perfectly. "After all, I want my maid of honor to really like the dress she has to wear and not toss it to the back of her closet never to look at again. So many attendants, I'm told, have to wear hideous dresses they hate."

"I love this dress," Suzanna purred and let the fabric of the skirt slide through her fingers. "Really. It's me." She hesitated and then turned to Sydney. "I know you had a little trouble at the party with Greta. But are you and Albert planning to invite her to the wedding."

"You must be kidding! After that whole terrible incident, why would we want her there?" Sydney pulled back with a stricken look on her face. "Why are you looking at me so funny? Do you think I should?"

"Actually, I was thinking of asking her to help serve punch and cake." Suzanna said the words slowly and peered over her large glasses at Sydney's shocked gasp.

"Now why would you do that? I can just imagine what will happen. My wedding day will be ruined. Is that what you want? A fight, or something even worse?" Sydney drew in a breath. "Oh. You think Greta has something to do with Edward's death. Is that it?"

"Yes I do. I can't tell you anything more at this time, but I have a feeling Greta knows something. I'm quite sure of it." Suzanna waited for an answer. She knew she was asking a lot of the bride-to-be. "I can't be sure things will be calm and uneventful, but I don't know when we will have all of these people in the same place again. I'm determined to solve Edward Garrett's murder. Are you?" Suzanna asked softly.

"Yes. I want this to be over. I don't want Albert to have this hanging over his head. Yes. You can ask Greta to serve cake. Is cake safe? Maybe it's better to have her at the cake table than at the punch bowl. Just make sure someone else cuts the cake. I would hate to think of her with a knife in her hand." They both howled. "And please, no black hooded cape. Supervise her attire."

The hotel was not big and beautiful – it was just an old fashioned neighborhood building tucked along the corner of a well traveled street. But the banquet room was large and provided an adequate space for a wedding. That Saturday afternoon was ideal. A lovely April day was something treasured by Minnesota natives. After a cold, blustering couple months of winter, the beginning of spring was anticipated with great relish.

Albert's mother bustled around the room making sure everything was just perfect. Her shrill voice barked out orders to the staff. "Let's straighten this cloth, Ella, please." And "Can we move this bouquet of flowers to a different corner? It's just too big for this spot." She proudly strutted around with a huge grin and a lot of fluttering hand gestures. Her flaming red hair and rotund body was difficult to miss. Planted in the middle of the room she gestured this way and then that way. Her constant chatter cut the quiet of the large almost empty room.

The wedding ceremony would begin at 5 pm with the reception immediately to follow. There was a retractable wall that would be removed when the dancing and dinner was to begin. The portable dance floor had been carefully shoved together and small tables circled the edges. Albert had, of course, hired the band. He couldn't wait to get up himself and play a few numbers for his friends and family.

Sydney sat in an small adjoining room. Her dress hung next to a floor length mirror propped in the corner. She sat at a table staring in a bag of make-up on its side with lipstick and brushes poking out. Peering at her face in a tiny illuminated mirror, she sighed. Make-up was something she hadn't bothered with until the studio. Edward Garrett's ex, Amanda had spent weeks helping her apply the stuff before it became second nature. Today she hoped she would remember all the tips Amanda had tried to implant. She stuck out her tongue and lifted her eyebrows up and down slowly as her nose pressed almost to the glassy surface of the mirror.

The road to this day had been long yet short. It had happened quickly, yet through the process one man had been murdered and someone was hiding a desperate secret – a secret that could be revealed tonight. Sydney didn't know which she was most worried about – the wedding itself or the possible revelation of a murderer.

"Are you ready for this?" Suzanna arrived with her dress in hand. She let her gaze scan the room, hung her dress, and took a seat across from Sydney. The quiet was deadening. Then she caught Sydney's eye. "Don't worry, everything will be just fine. How are you feeling? You aren't nervous, are you?"

Sydney just smiled. When she didn't answer, Suzanna continued. "The room looks lovely. I peeked in before I came in here. Your soon to be mother-in-law was taking care of everything. This will be a very nice evening. I promise…really." Suzanna tapped her berry colored nails on the top of the table and pulled up her shoulder bag to unload her own make-up case and hair brush.

"Did you see Albert?" Sydney's voice was thin and timid.

"I spotted him running around with his usual burst of energy as he helped the band carry in stands and music stuff. He was in his glory, believe me. And he looked very handsome, I might add. Of course, not as handsome as Sheldon." Suzanna chose her words carefully and blushed a crimson red. She wanted the mood to be upbeat and worry free. She knew there was the possibility things could turn upside down tonight and inside she felt sorry it had to happen this way. But it couldn't be helped.

"You and Sheldon seem to be getting closer," Sydney commented. "What's going on with relationship, huh Suzanna?" Her voice began to take on a teasing tone. It broke the tension in the room.

"I guess you could say it is getting more serious than I had anticipated." Suzanna hummed as she snatched up her dress and headed to the rest room to change.

Sydney fingered the lace of her dress. It might be cheap, but it certainly was as perfect as she could imagine a wedding dress could be. Slipping into the gown she actually began to feel the part of a bride. There she said it to herself, "bride". The word had terrified her up until this very moment. Today she seemed to settle into the role quite nicely. As she gazed at herself in the mirror, she smiled. Twirling from side to side so the lace skirt swirled around her legs, she clasped her arms around herself and fingered lightly the shoulder ruffle.

Suzanna appeared behind her peering over her round glasses. "You look wonderful. How is this?" She grasped the fabric from behind and extended the skirt as she spun just as she would if dancing a Viennese Waltz. The edges of the dress fluttered softly.

"Gorgeous!" Sydney beamed. "Now for my make-up and hair." She sat down again at the table and stared into the mirror.

A light rap at the door interrupted her thoughts. "Dear," came the raspy voice of Albert's father. "Would you like me to do your hair?"

Sydney jumped to her feet and pulled open the door. "You are a life saver! Thank you so much," she sighed.

Albert's father carefully arranged both Sydney's and Suzanna's hair and even helped them apply their make-up. "How did you know?" Sydney gave him a quick hug. Without even looking into his face, she could sense his pride. His body exuded an energy that created a delightful feeling in the room. "Thank you," she whispered.

The wedding was beautiful. Short but beautiful. Sydney and Suzanna walked slowly down the aisle as the faces of guests turned to observe the procession. Albert stood at the end with Cary standing beside him. Cary teetered nervously but Albert was beaming confidently.

When the ceremony was over, the hotel workers quickly opened the dividing wall and pushed and pulled tables into place. Sydney, Albert, Suzanna and Cary joined the family in a receiving line at the entrance to the ballroom. Greta sauntered in and took her place with Angie behind the table with the cake. Servers had cut the second cake and put small iced slices on plates on one end of the table while the traditional cake topped with the figures of a bride and groom was on the other end. Greta looked very normal but seemed in an unusually sour mood. Dressed in a simple navy blue short sleeve dress with matching pumps and a circle of pearls at her throat, Greta looked as if she could blend right in with the crowd. She snapped at Angie when she apparently stood at the wrong end of the table. Then she picked up a plate of cake and peering more closely at the sugary frosting quickly slapped it back down on the table rolling her eyes.

Mary Lou was at the other end of the room clinging to Larry Underhill's arm. She was dressed in a black and white patterned shirt dress with low black dance shoes. Larry was his usual dapper self in an elegant gray suit with a tiny yellow rose bud on the lapel. It was an obvious attempt to wear his usual flower without taking away from the wedding party. Mary Lou glanced over toward Greta behind the cake table. Suzanna had warned her Greta would be there, but assured her that she would be given a duty preventing her from mingling with the other guests. Greta scanned the room and stopped to stare at the pair in the corner. She glared for a second and then with a sly grin moved her eyes to another part of the room. Mary Lou squirmed and clutched Larry's arm a little tighter.

Larry motioned for Mary Lou to follow him toward the middle of the dance floor. She tried to hold him back, but he seemed determined to speak with someone in the center of the room. The band was beginning to set up equipment and tuning instruments as people milled around in small groups to chat. Antoine was standing with Sheila and Morgan watching the band. He bounced anxiously at the tuning ritual, tapping his foot to the sporadic beat.

Suddenly, two men in basic black suits moved in to clamp hands on Larry Underhill. Mary Lou was roughly brushed aside. Antoine Hawks snatched her back into the crowd as the men pronounced Larry under arrest for the murder of Edward Garrett. Mary Lou's mouth gaped in surprise. Antoine focused his attention on Mary Lou as she slumped weakly into his arms.

Larry turned his head back and forth in shocking surprise as the men asked him to put his hands behind his back. Suddenly, Greta Rothe leaped from behind the cake table as quickly as a cat pouncing on a mouse. She slammed her body into one of the men knocking the handcuffs from his hands.

"Run!" She hissed at Larry. "Get out of here." She expertly positioned her body so the men were just out of reach of Larry Underhill. Just as quickly, two more men surrounded both Larry and Greta with guns drawn. "He didn't kill Edward Garrett," Greta snarled twirling to view the circling men. "I did." Greta was in a tense martial arts pose, hands out and legs crouched ready to swing out a protective kick. Her movements were in slow motion and controlled.

"Oh, we know that," one of the men purred smoothly. They nodded to Larry Underhill. "You can go back to the wedding party if you like," he motioned with a head nod to Larry. "We know you didn't kill Mr. Garrett.

Sorry about all of the drama, but we needed to catch this one by surprise and get some sort of acknowledgement from her about them murder."

"So I was bait?" Larry Underhill never showed anything but charm, but at this moment he was bristling with anger.

Greta struggled slightly, but quickly calmed submissively when she realized she was surrounded. "Sorry," the man apologized again as they cuffed Greta and walked her out of the room. Her last look was an angry glare back over her shoulder at Mary Lou, still supported by Antoine Hawks. Mary Lou shivered. Then in an angry twist, she nodded her head toward Larry Underhill and announced "You just got a freebee, mister."

Suzanna motioned to the dance staff to join her in the corner of the ballroom. They quickly clustered together straining and eager to find out exactly what was going on. Larry Underhill moved along with group and elbowed his way forward to meet Suzanna face to face.

"Explain to me what just happened here," he demanded. His eyes no longer sparkled. They glared.

Suzanna explained that Greta Rothe had always been somewhat of a mystery to everyone in the dance studio. Rumors of her involvement as a private eye or CIA agent got her thinking. The police had arrested Albert initially because of some type of clue left by Edward Garrett at Tara. Sydney and Suzanna had discovered something was left on the floor or written by Edward as he was dying. They began to suspect it was a name or initials written in blood on the glass dance floor. The police had suspected Albert, but somehow the name "Albert" or "Rothchild" seemed too long for a dying man to write. So they decided it might be initials. "AR". Who would have those initials? Well, LARry might work. But then they couldn't imagine what motive Larry Underhill would have to murder Edward. Antoine had mentioned he saw Larry meeting with Greta outside of the studio, and when Greta threatened Mary Lou, the only reason anyone could come up with was some sort of involvement between Greta and Larry. Mary Lou appeared to be very socially involved with Larry. After Greta threatened Mary Lou, Suzanna had decided to dig into Greta's past a bit more. She contacted the police and in outlining her suspicions discovered the word written on the floor was "ROTH". The police only had the name of "Rothchild" on the list of dancers at the Tara photo shoot. Greta Rothe was never listed anywhere as a suspect. When Suzanna brought up her name, they discovered something very interesting about Greta. She was a suspected contract killer. Yes, she was an interesting character, but it wasn't on the side of the CIA or FBI. She was a hired assassin. They had to find out if Larry had hired Greta or if Greta was working on her own.

"Larry, your surprise at being a suspect was what we needed. Then when Greta ran out to protect you, we realized you were an innocent person in this whole affair. You were as confused as everyone else in the room except Greta Rothe." Suzanna nodded at Larry. He bit his lip and after a moment of thought broke into his usual grin.

"I did meet with Greta, but I didn't have any idea she was so unusual. She actually asked me lots of questions about the billboard and photo shoot. I'm afraid I related some anxiety about Edward not paying me on time. I must have seemed very desperate just then. I guess she had become more attached to me than I realize, and she decided to take action the only way she knew how. I suppose she thought Edward's death would get me my money. It was quite a chunk, and I let her know I really was in bad shape until he paid up. I'm afraid that was a mistake on my part. She made some pretty strange remarks that actually made me quite angry the last time we met. I even got up and left the restaurant because she was reacting with such hostility. It was a bit unsettling – like seeing Dr.

Jekyl and Mr. Hyde." Larry shook his head as he thought back on what he had noticed. "I should have kept things much more professional and not confided in her. But I had no idea she was someone who murdered people for a living." He frowned. "And I certainly had no idea I was putting both Edward Garrett and Mary Lou in danger."

"Well, no one did," Suzanna added. "If Greta's name hadn't suddenly come up in my conversation with the police, I doubt if we would have known she was under investigation for other crimes. This was the case that broke open that investigation completely. We were trying to find some way to get some truth, and I'm afraid we had to use a wedding to do it." Suzanna nodded to Sydney and Albert. "I'm sorry we had to spoil your day."

"Are you kidding?" Sydney beamed. "I was hoping we could clear Albert before the wedding, but during…just as good. And who said this was spoiled? Let's get back to the party and enjoy the rest of the day, shall we?" She looked around the huddled group and was met with host of "yeah" and "let's go". They motioned for the band to begin and within moments, the dance floor was crowded.

Suzanna and Sheldon were swaying slowly to a fast song as they cornered Sydney. Albert was at the front of the band playing away on his violin, sweat glistening on his forehead. The three stopped for a moment and listened. "Are you sure this didn't ruin your wedding day?" Suzanna quietly whispered in Sydney's ear.

"No. I wish I had known what was planned, but I know you couldn't bring people into your confidence with so much at stake. I'm really surprised at the outcome. I didn't even think about Greta. I guess we all thought of her as just an innocent nut case. She always was odd, but that was probably what she wanted people to think. It was a perfect disguise to be slightly off balance. Everyone avoided her. How perfect!" Sydney tried to think back about her encounters with Greta and began to understand some of the strange characteristics she had shown. The puzzle was beginning to fit into place.

"I feel relieved. Relieved." She smiled and fluttered her fingers at Albert who nodded and smiled. "Very relieved." The day was good – and she was about to begin the start of a whirlwind new life. She smiled.

Hustle Basic:

Man's part: Starting with the left foot move side together side (count 1,2,3), Tap with the right foot with no weight (count 4), Move back to the right with a side together side (count 1,2,3), Tap with the left foot with no weight (count 4). Repeat. This pattern may also be danced forward and backward.

Lady's part: Starting with the right foot move side together side (count 1,2,3), Tap with the left foot with no weight (count 4), Move back to the left with a side together side (count 1,2,3), Tap with the right foot with no weight (count 4). Repeat. This pattern may also be danced forward and backward.